Challenge of the Barons

Lekan Are

UNIVERSITY PRESS PLC
IBADAN
2001

University Press PLC
IBADAN ABA ABUJA AKURE BENIN ILORIN JOS KANO
LAGOS MAIDUGURI ONITSHA OWERRI ZARIA

ISBN 978 030251 4

First Published in the U.S.A. by Vintage Press Inc. 1977
First Published by University Press PLC 1995

New Impression 2001

Printed by: FOLUDEX PRESS LTD. IB.
Published by University Press PLC
Three Crowns Building, Jericho, P.M.B. 5095, Ibadan, Nigeria
Fax 02-2412056 E-mail: unipress@skannet.com.ng

Challenge of the Barons

To the future of my children
OLUFUNKE, AYOKUNNU AND ADEDAMOLA

Be prepared!

Challenge of the Barons is purely imaginative. The persons and organizations described are imaginary. Any sarcasm apparently directed at any known person or organization is purely coincidental and therefore unintentional.

–Lekan Are
Ibadan, Nigeria

1

DEPARTURE FROM NIGERIA

The announcement was made on the radio at five o'clock in the morning. Not many listeners in Ibadan tune in for the five o'clock news. It is far too early for most of them. At the Jungu home, life begins at six o'clock every morning, and this was typical of middle-class homes in Ibadan. It was Monday morning and the Jungus had had quite a hectic Sunday. Dr Onaola Jungu, his wife Aida, and their two sons Olu and Bunmi had been out visiting relations in Gbongan some sixty kilometres from Ibadan. They had returned late on Sunday, tired and exhausted. Dr Jungu had gone to bed that night promising himself that he would have a long lie-in in the morning and get into the office a little late. This was not to be.

As the first morning light struggled through the fine pores of the *adire* curtains in their bedroom and stirred Aida into consciousness, the telephone rang.

'What a nuisance,' growled Aida; then, half awake, she clutched the receiver.

'48514, Aida Jungu,' she mumbled.

Over the line came a booming:

'Congratulations and best wishes for Onaola's new job. Put me on to him, please; Segun here.'

Covering the mouthpiece of the telephone, Aida gave her husband a gentle nudge.

'Uh, uh.'

'Come on, it's Segun.'

In a hardly audible voice, he objected.

'No calls, please I am dead beat, you know that.'

'It's Segun, Cousin Segun. You must take it, just a brief word with him. That's all and you can go back to sleep.'

'Sleep! You've wrecked it already.'

'Segun, he's here; just hold on a minute.' Aida spoke into the receiver.

Unwillingly grabbing the telephone receiver, Dr Jungu yelled:

'What's so urgent, man! One cannot have a decent sleep in this place.'

'Boy, oh boy, what's eating you? Congratulations! It came on the air at five o'clock this morning.'

'What. . . ?'

'Your new appointment. Didn't you hear it?'

'Of course I didn't.'

'Good heavens, cheer up; you should be in high spirits. Professor!'

'What Professor? I don't know what you are talking about. Honestly, Segun, I have still not recovered from our visit yesterday to Gbongan. We spent the day with Mama Jide and the Afolabis, and you know what that means. Driving on that terrible road is bad enough, but being taken round to see friends of a friend and relations of a relation and then being forced to eat seven lunches in one afternoon just beats me!'

'Ah well, that's life, but aren't you lucky? You will soon be temporarily out of it all.'

'What are you getting at, Segun?' he asked, trying to evade the issue.

2

'Since when have you been thinking of taking up a job at Serti University? This is unlike you; you seem to have kept your plans all to yourself this time.'

Dr Jungu was surprised that the news had leaked out. The offer of a Professorship and chairmanship of the Department of Horticulture at Serti University had been a closely guarded secret. He had accepted the offer just over a month ago and was waiting for the right psychological moment to break the news to his relations and friends. There was now no need to hide anything. To Aida, however, it was stale news.

'OK, Cousin Segun. It was all done quietly. You know how it is around here. You cannot shout out loud on a thing like this before it comes through.'

'Anyway, congratulations again, and the best of luck.'

'Thank you.' Dr Jungu replaced the receiver on its cradle.

Aida was happy that the news was out at last. Her husband had broken it to her three weeks earlier, but now it was different. Everyone would soon know about it and about their new status. She hugged him and congratulated him warmly.

'Good Lord, it's like I am hearing it for the first time. I am so happy for you, darling.'

'Thank you, Aida. I am glad too.'

The telephone rang ceaselessly that morning. Each time Dr Jungu picked it up, he heard the same word: 'Congratulations!' The news was travelling fast and it was getting more and more embarrassing to say, 'Thank you, nice of you to have rung.'

Dr Jungu took his bath later than usual. He had to rush through it to get to work by eight o'clock. His office was located at the southeast end of Ibadan, only half a kilometre from his house.

Ibadan is a very big city by African standards. It has a population more than one million and is located not particularly far from Lagos, the former capital of the Federal Republic of Nigeria, one of the fastest-growing countries in Africa. Lagos, otherwise called Eko, is a busy seaport city under one hundred and forty kilometres away.

Ibadan was for very many years a renowned trading outpost. Its affairs were creditably managed by mature reputable chiefs, popularly referred to as the 'city fathers.' Their average age was between sixty five and eighty. Most of these chiefs were illiterate. They, however, learnt the art of governing their people through a well-organized system of learning on the job. Illiteracy had been rampant amongst its teeming population, but the rapid expansion of western education since Nigeria attained independence quickly changed the situation and Ibadan has been, more receptive to these changes than many other cities in Nigeria. It has become the proud home of a university, a higher teachers' college, a school of agriculture and forestry and numerous secondary and primary schools. With time, the young people of Ibadan took full advantage of these educational facilities. After twelve years of independence, four out of every five young persons in Ibadan had benefitted from primary education, while about a quarter of all children of school age had also enjoyed secondary education. This was a remarkable achievement.

The Ibadan Forestry Department where Dr Jungu worked employed thirty-five African scientists, all of them products of Ibadan. On arrival at the office, he found that almost the entire staff of the department where he was assistant chief forester had gathered close to the entrance of the staircase leading to his office. He was besieged by all and sundry. The crowd shouted congratulations in unison as if it had been previously rehearsed. He took his time to shake hands with everyone. His fingers were almost crushed by the pressure exerted by the firm grip of the enthusiastic crowd, and he thanked his stars when it was all over. As he watched the crowd disperse, his secretary Bertie, who had just arrived, ran to him and shouted 'Congratulations, sir, I rejoice with you over your merited elevation.'

'Thank you for your kind sentiments.'

'But why Serti if I may ask, sir?'

'Come with me to the office. It's a long story.'

As they walked along the verandah and later up the staircase to Dr Jungu's office, a few workers still lined the route saying congratulations. In his office, he explained to Bertie that he considered it an honour to go out and serve in Serti. After all, Serti was in the Democratic Republic of Kato and Kato people, as she should know, have had over a century of contact with western civilization, serving in Nigeria for over fifty years as clerks and teachers when Nigeria lacked personnel in these fields. He noted that now, when Kato needed the services of experienced, qualified people in various fields, it should be considered a worthy endeavour for citizens of Nigeria to offer their services to her. Kato was another independent African country just like his native Nigeria and working there would be a way of making his contribution to the promotion of the much publicized African unity.

'But, sir do you think Kato people will treat you like one of them?' asked Bertie.

'Poor you, an African ought to be respected in another sister African country. I don't expect discriminatory practices there.'

5

'But, sir, you may say you are black and proud. That's in theory. Nigerians are Nigerians and Kato men are Kato men. Your experiences may yet prove me right.'

'Bertie, we must call a halt to this unproductive exchange. I hope you realize that I am still in the service of the Ibadan Forestry Department. I must justify the day's pay. Any urgent matters pending? Which appointments do I have today?'

Bertie drooped her head and walked out of Dr Jungu's office shutting the door behind her.

It was three years ago or so when Bertie first met her boss, a man she had come to admire and respect. She remembered her first contact with him. It came back quite vividly to her. Chief Forester Mr Donga had introduced her to Dr Jungu. 'Meet your new secretary. Her name is Bertie Ajanta.'

He gave her a warm handshake as he said, 'Pleased to meet you.' As Mr Donga took leave of them, she was offered a seat and Dr Jungu spoke slowly and advised as follows. 'You are but a young girl. Take your work seriously and avoid bad company. Be punctual and be prepared to make sacrifices in the interest of your job and the department. You may have to do overtime occasionally. This is referred to as 'overdash' by our people.'

'Is that because no one ever gets paid for it?' Bertie remembered asking.

'Certainly not. It is not a 'dash' for all that I know. These little extra contributions might tilt the balance in your favour on that fateful day when you are to be considered for advancement. Our people refer to this as the day of reckoning. Work diligently whether I am around or not. You must show that your output can be really high without supervision and

6

that you can be relied upon at all times. In addition, read over whatever you are asked to type, correct any mistakes either emanating from your fingers or due to an error of my head.'

She remembered bursting into a fit of laughter on hearing that a man of Dr Jungu's seniority and experience could make mistakes too.

'Young lady, may I continue?'

Dr Jungu had rattled on for an additional twenty minutes and, to crown it all, he emphasized that he would always call her attention to her misdemeanours verbally and that should she repeat the same mistakes after repeated correction, he might lose his temper with her and would certainly shout at her. He reminded her however, that it would be over, there and then.

'I will smile with you but that should not be taken as license for slackness. My guiding principles have been to be fair, friendly, but firm with those who work with me. I assure you of a most rewarding and satisfying tenure of office in this department. Also, you must remember at all times to keep our secrets secret. All the best,' Dr Jungu had stopped abruptly.

Bertie remembered saying, 'Thank you, sir, I pray to live up to your expectations.'

Bertie found that her boss would scold her like she was his sister whenever she was adjudged to have done something improper, but he did not fail to shower praises on her whenever she did her job well. She remembered clearly the day Dr Jungu shouted at her for failing to lock his cabinet for three days in a row even though he had given his usual three warnings. Bertie recalled that she trembled, thinking the end had come. She recollected that some thirty minutes later when she brought the draft of a tour report, Dr Jungu was full of praise because she had inserted the words 'had been' in the appropriate place on her own initiative. She realized there and then that her boss did not hold a grudge against anyone and was a most wonderful person once he was understood. This had taken a few months. She also found that it took a short time to understand that he was very straightforward and that he was the darling of most of the members of staff, junior and senior. As she continued to reflect on her past working association with Dr Jungu, the telephone rang. 'Sir, anything?' Bertie said, shaking herself from her daydream. Dr Jungu was on the other end of the line.

'Bertie! I am still waiting for you to bring the day's assignments.'

'Pardon me, I will be with you in a minute, sir,' replied Bertie.

Bertie dropped the telephone gently, opened her diary, and scanned very quickly through her jottings, which read as follows:

9:00 a.m.	Discussion with Mr Mutairu of Topa Chemicals.
11:00 a.m.	Expecting Professor Aditu of the University of Ibadan.
12:00 noon	Heads of Departments meeting.
5: 00 p.m.	Football match at Olubadan Stadium.

'Sir, you will have quite a busy day today. I will bring in a copy of the programme.'

'Uh! It's a busy day indeed.'

Many days rolled by, and to Jungu's relief, the news of his

8

impending departure seemed to have died down, until one afternoon, Bertie announced the arrival of the secretary of the Junior Staff Workers Union accompanied by the president and three other members of the executive. There had been no appointment made.

'Would you have time to see them, sir?'

'Let them come in. I hope they are here for official consultation,' replied Dr Jungu.

Bertie opened the door and ushered them in.

'How are you all today?' greeted Dr Jungu.

The secretary, Mr Jonjo Brukus, replied instantly as if it were a command. 'Bad, and I assure you this is the feeling of those that we represent and all the members of our executive.'

Dr Jungu asked Bertie to bring in more chairs and invited everyone to sit down.

'Now that you are seated, may I ask whether you have come to demand another pay rise?' he asked smilingly, because they did not exchange the usual African salutation. Dr Jungu was not quite at ease since he could not read their minds. Mr Jonjo Brukus spoke on behalf of the five members of the union present:

'Our dear brother, Jungu, we will be deceiving you if we tell you that we are happy about your impending departure from among us. I assure you, we are not. This is why we are here today–to convey to you a big wish from our union members. We have had a meeting and our view is that you should not resign. We have benefitted from time to time from your advice and assurances, especially over crucial staff matters. We do not feel that all will be well with us when you leave us. We prefer to be with a man who keeps his promise and like our fathers say, whose 'yes' is 'yes' and of course whose 'no' is

9

'no.' Many of our members have made phenomenal progress in this department with your assistance. Do not leave us to suffer, as we may not have another man like you as your replacement. We know that we cannot tie you down and we hesitate to impede your personal progress in life. I am in fact asked to appeal to you to make a big sacrifice for our sake by rejecting your new offer of appointment as Professor and head of the Department of Horticulture at Serti University. This is our humble request.'

In the customary African way, the president of the union felt that he might not be doing justice to his exalted position if he did not put in a word. So he rose with an elder's dignity and said solemnly:

'Our dear brother, you have listened attentively to the words of our able secretary who has crystallized our views. I wish to add only a few words not necessarily new ideas. You will realize that this is the way we tend to repeat the same thing over and over, hoping that it will sink. We will miss you should you decide to go to Serti in Kato. We don't want you to go. We were afraid to come to you earlier for fear that you might not be prepared to listen to us, especially as you appeared to us to be very happy over the appointment. I must assure you that we feel personally pleased with your elevation and are convinced that it is in appreciation of your professional contributions. As hinted by Jonjo, ours is a selfish motive for wanting you to stay. It is for self-preservation. We believe strongly that when you leave, a lot of us will begin to suffer, as we will no longer get what we deserve. You have been our saviour to date. We therefore implore you to consider withdrawing your resignation and stay with us.'

'Is that all?' asked Dr Jungu as Mr. Batolo, the president, sank gracefully but slowly into his seat.

'Yes, and I don't think anyone wants to add to what I have said.'

Dr Jungu thanked the executive of the Junior Staff Workers Union and its members for all the nice things said about him. He prayed that he might be lucky to have dedicated people like them in Serti. As regards their request, he explained that it was rather late to withdraw his resignation. He explained that this was firstly because he had given his notice three months ago. Secondly, he held the view that should he back out at that stage after having assured the authorities at Serti that he would accept the offer, this might ruin the chances of other citizens of Nigeria who might wish to seek high posts in Kato. He explained further that he was convinced that life would go on pleasantly for them without him and that many of them would still make good. He advised that if they really had regard for him, they should wish him well and not attempt to persuade him to reverse his decision. In any case, he felt he had already reached the point of no return. He thanked them once again for the interest that they had in him and prayed that they might have a much better man to step into his shoes.

The representatives of the union made one last effort to persuade Dr Jungu, but Jungu stood his ground. Finding that their mission had failed to achieve its primary objective, they begged to take leave of him. As they passed through Bertie's cubicle, she asked. 'I hope you managed to persuade him to stay with us.'

Jonjo was quick to retort. 'You know our man Jungu. He was frank and blunt as always. You can trust him; his mind is already made up to leave. I assure you no one else can change his mind, not even his mother or father. This is one of his good qualities - always straightforward. How we wish he would change his mind and remain with us.'

'Well,' said Bertie, 'perhaps we are asking too much of him. A man like Dr Jungu is too good and too clever to be kept locked up here. I am told that he had an outstanding academic record. My father said he was born and raised here at Ibadan. He thinks he must be forty years old. He was a product of two illustrious families. His father was from a stock of veteran warriors in the Ibadan of yesteryear, while his mother hailed from a family of respectable Christian people. Because of the strong influence of his maternal grandmother who was a fanatical Christian, he had attended a missionary primary school. He was lucky to enjoy the privilege of secondary education in his time. This was a rare privilege then as most children's educational ambition was halted after six years of primary education, since only two schools in Ibadan offered the opportunity to attend the last two classes at the primary level—Christ Church School, Mapo and Government School, Kings Barracks, Ibadan later known as N.A. Central School. The competition to gain admission into the last two classes—standards five and six—was very keen. All the pupils in standard four had to take the examinations for just sixty places annually: thirty pupils being admitted into each of the two select schools. Father said that Dr Jungu gained admission into the Ibadan Native Authority School where he read for his standards five and six certificates.

'I think Father admires him. He believes that he is a sober man, although inquisitive. He was a brilliant pupil who shone like a bright star. He won a Nigerian National Secondary School scholarship. Later, he attended the Government Secondary School located at the southeastern end of Ibadan. It was reputedly the best secondary school of the land. He later gained admission into the University of Western Nigeria—you know that is right here in Ibadan. After five years he obtained the B.Sc. in Forestry and joined the Ibadan Forestry Department. After a year of field experience, he travelled to the United States of America where he obtained the M.Sc. and Ph.D. degrees in horticulture having specialized in post-harvest physiology.'

The representatives listened with rapt attention to Bertie. Before she could say all she wanted, Jonjo cut in. 'We know about him here, too. He is the most honest senior staff we know. He is hard-working and has a pleasant disposition. He rose to the position of assistant chief forester in this department, after only seven years' meritorious service. We know he talks a lot, but he is a good mixer with excellent public relations. He is argumentative and often tries to get people to see things from his own point of view. Mr Donga, the chief forester, always says that you cannot joke with Jungu because of his memory. He could quote dates of events of yesteryear with fantastic precision to drive home his point. We all know he makes friends very easily and he is always frank and blunt. Many people wish he were a bit more diplomatic though, as he lives in an age where people prefer deceit to being told the truth.'

Batolo then added: 'Dr Jungu was also a distinguished sportsman with a special flair for football, table tennis, and cricket. He won secondary school and university honours in the three games and represented Ibadan Football Association in many important football matches. You must see his house. It is an archive of many trophies and medals won on the field of play. After his many years of association with football, he was invited to serve as a member of the Ibadan Football Association. He served the association in various capacities, including that of vice- president.'

13

Jonjo Brukus had to stop the gossip. 'Let us get away from here. The rest of the staff are waiting.' Sorrowful expressions appeared boldly written on the faces of the five executive members of the Junior Staff Workers Union. As they approached many of their members who had gathered beneath a mango tree near the office, sensed that the mission had failed.

'What happened?' asked an impatient member of the union who went by the name of Mr Alimamy.

'Silence,' blared out Jonjo Brukus, the able and respected union secretary. 'I regret to inform you that we were unsuccessful in our mission. Try hard as we did, our beloved Dr Jungu stood his ground. I assure you we were as usual impressed by his frankness. Let us face realities and chart a new course. Let us contribute generously and give him a most worthy send-off party and a memorable parting gift. We shall miss him, no doubt; but remember, this was bound to happen one day. So we had better learn to live without his wise counsel. We, your executive, will put our heads together and come up with useful proposals for the send-off party in another week. We trust that you will support us and show in a big way that Dr Jungu is indeed our man.'

There was dead silence as Mr Brukus finished his speech. The crowd left one by one, apparently unhappy that the union was unable to convince Dr Jungu to remain at Ibadan

Six weeks before his departure, send-off parties were held every day of the week. It was unbelievable. No one else who had ever worked at Ibadan Forestry Department had been so lavishly honoured. The Board of Directors of the department with all the chief foresters- from the nooks and crannies of the Federal Republic of Nigeria turned up for the first party. It

14

was impossible to name all the groups or individuals that arranged parties in honour of Dr Jungu. Suffice to say that they included the entire staff of Ibadan Forestry Department, the Junior Staff Workers Union, Dr Jungu's section of the department, the chief forester in his private capacity, sporting organizations at Ibadan, university dons, and individual staff members of Ibadan Forestry Department. There was even a fantastic civic send-off party given by the chiefs and citizens of Ibadan.

Dr and Mrs Jungu were worn out by the time they left Ibadan, their only consolation being that they were assured of a good rest during the four-day boat trip to Kato. As they left Ibadan for Eko, where Dr Jungu and his family were to board the boat, many of the workers from the Ibadan Forestry Department who had gathered to see them off wept openly. Dr Jungu waved goodbye as the car taking them to Eko pulled out gradually. Mrs Jungu and the rest of the family looked back and waved. They had with them their faithful watchdog, Shole.

2

VOYAGE TO BUKTU

Dr Jungu and his family arrived at Eko after a four-hour car ride. The driver was slow, because he had to avoid a great number of potholes on the so-called first-class road on which they travelled. He drove the Jungus straight to the house of Mr Ayinde Ologun the first cousin of Dr Jungu. Mrs Filo Ologun was outside to welcome them.

'How was the journey? I hope you had a nice trip?' asked Mrs Ologun as she embraced Aida.

'Filo, I am sorry to have kept you waiting for quite a long time. We were unlucky to have had a punctured tyre, hence the delay,' explained Aida.

'No wonder!' replied Filo. 'Ayinde had to leave for an appointment thirty minutes ago. We both expected you around three o'clock, an hour earlier than now.'

Mrs Ologun, noting that the members of the Jungu family were perspiring profusely, led them upstairs where two air-conditioned rooms were reserved for them, one for Dr Jungu and Aida, the other for their children, Olu and Bunmi. Shole, ever vigilant and faithful, followed them into the rooms wagging her tail. She was indeed a lovely little dog.

Dr Jungu set out early the next morning to take Shole to a veterinary doctor for vaccination and a note to certify that she was fit and well to travel. Then he decided to see the sales manager of Kintu shipping lines. Only cargo boats were available, but the date of sailing from Eko would not be known until the boats were almost fully loaded. The manager gave Dr Jungu his telephone number and advised that he should be contacted fairly regularly.

That evening Dr Zannu, the veterinary doctor, called on the Jungus to assure himself that the shots given to Shole had not upset her. Shole was rather drowsy throughout the day, but seemed to have overcome the side effect by evening. Shole jumped at Dr Zannu and wagged her tail vigorously. Not long after, as Dr Zannu was leaving, he suggested that he would like to introduce the Jungus to his business partner who lived a few blocks from them, just in case his services were needed. Dr Jungu and his wife drove after Dr Zannu's car. Shole ran after both cars, probably thinking that they were returning to Ibadan. The Jungus returned to the house of Mr Ologun close to midnight and Shole was nowhere to be found. A search was organized the next day for her, but it was unsuccessful.

'But where is Shole?' asked Bunmi.

'I am afraid she is probably lost,' replied Dr Jungu.

'Please go and get her or we won't eat.'

'I assure you efforts will be made to find her.'

Olu and Bunmi became terribly upset, and for once all members of the Jungu family began to appreciate their close attachment to their dog. The children prayed that the boat would not be ready for another four to five days in the hope that she might be found before then.

Before Dr Jungu returned home the next day, the manager of Kintu Shipping Lines had sent an urgent message that the boat was to leave at six o'clock in the evening of the following day and that reporting time was three o'clock in the afternoon. He added that unless the Jungus had their cholera shots, they could not travel. Dr Jungu was enraged at this threat. He picked up the telephone and complained that it might be difficult to comply with this request. Later that evening Dr Oloyede called on the Jungus and he was apprised of their dilemma. He offered to help and gladly drove the Jungus to his clinic where he gave them cholera shots and recorded same in their health certificate.

'But Daddy, isn't it time to look for Shole again?' asked the children.

Feeling that the children's priorities were misplaced, Dr Jungu promised to go round the neighbourhood that evening. To please them, he undertook yet another search, which again proved fruitless. Looking sad and displeased on returning, he advised that everyone should go to bed. It was barely six o'clock the next morning when a joyous shout was heard from the children. Dr Jungu and his wife rushed out to check on what had happened.

'Shole has returned,' shouted the children in unison.

In spite of their doubts, the Jungus could not but go downstairs to check on what their children had seen. Halfway up the staircase they met with the children carrying Shole, who wagged her tail as an expression of great joy.

'A pleasant surprise, isn't it?' stated Olu.

Shole's hair was stroked and she murmured for joy as she rolled on the floor and wagged her tail still more vigorously. The children took Shole with them, gave her a good bath, and dried her hair with a towel. They rejoiced all that morning at the unexpected reunion.

By noon, a truck had arrived to carry the luggage of the Jungus to the wharf. Just about the same time, eight members of staff of the Ibadan Forestry Department arrived to load the truck. It was as if it were prearranged. For one thing it was a Saturday, a nonworking day since they operated on a five-day week at Ibadan. Dr Jungu's friends from Ibadan were glad they could help. They had only come to see him and his family and were not aware that they were to travel that day. What a happy coincidence that they could bid them goodbye!

The sun was high. The men sweated and sang a popular old school song. 'Happy days are here again,' as they passed the luggage from one to the other. By two o'clock in the afternoon, they had accomplished their task. They were not keen on having lunch, but did not fail to cool down with what one of them described as criminally cold beer.

At a quarter past two, Dr Jungu announced that it was time to leave for the wharf. He seized the opportunity to acknowledge the assistance rendered by his eight friends from Ibadan and praised them for sacrificing so much to see his family off. He promised to write to every one of them after settling down at Serti. He prayed for their advancement in life and wished them and their families the very best of luck and success. He shook hands with them one by one before leaving.

Mr Amusa Jungu, Onaola's uncle, gladly provided his car for the journey to the wharf. The car, followed by the truck, pulled out rather fast as the well-wishers waved goodbye. In addition to the Jungus, it carried Mr Amusa Jungu and Mrs Ayinde Ologun, the only two people to see them off.

On reaching the wharf, the luggage was checked in without much trouble. It turned out that apart from deck passengers, the Jungus were the only other passengers on this cargo boat MV Mopti. They were in the first-class cabin. Dr and Mrs Jungu were allocated a double room while a single room each was made available to their two children. As they were making for their rooms on the boat, one of the officers suddenly realized that Shole was accompanying them.

'Excuse me, sir,' said the sailor.

'Are you taking this pet along with you on this trip? I need to see its travel papers for verification.' Sensing that Shole might run into more trouble, Dr Jungu opened his briefcase and brought out the veterinary certificates issued on her. The officer inspected them and queried whether Shole had a ticket for the journey. He advised Dr Jungu to go to the wharf office of the Kintu Shipping Lines to pay twenty-five dollars for her trip. Meanwhile Aida and the children had been conducted to their rooms by two other sailors.

Just as it appeared that everything was finally in order, there was a tap on the door of Room 2- the double room of Dr and Mrs Jungu.

'Come in if you are good-looking,' said Dr Jungu jokingly.

As the door swung open, in came Mr Hill, a burly, tough-looking male who turned out to be the captain of the boat.

'Good evening, lady and gentleman,' greeted Mr Hill.

'I understand you have a dog on board. We have strict instructions not to carry unvaccinated animals.'

Mr Hill had only barely finished talking when Dr. Jungu cut in.

'Have you not been told by one of your officers who accosted us some two hours ago that the dog is duly vaccinated and that we have veterinary certificates to show?'

Mr Hill calmed him down, saying that he was aware of this, but that he had fears that the dog had probably not been given the cholera shot.

Dr Jungu, becoming furious shouted in dismay: 'Cholera shot for a dog, I thought they were reserved for humans and not for poor lower animals.'

20

Mr Hill appealed to him to calm down. He explained that since the boat was no longer sailing that evening, he felt that there was enough time to sort things out with the shipping authorities early the following morning. He suggested that the dog be kept off the boat till the next morning. Dr Jungu accepted the suggestion half-heartedly, but with a proviso that the captain would be personally responsible for her well-being.

'Leave her to me. She is in good hands,' assured Mr Hill. Shole was handed over to Mr Hill. She followed protestingly.

Olu and Bunmi complained about the rough treatment Shole was being subjected to. They followed the captain everywhere he went, chanting:

'Give us our dog. It has suffered enough.'

Though embarrassed, Mr Hill tried his best to explain matters to the children, but he did not succeed in convincing them that his action was justifiable.

Mr Amusa Jungu, being a self-employed man, bid Dr Jungu and his family goodbye and left for his shop to close up for the day. The Jungus, however, insisted on Mrs Ayinde Ologun having dinner with them on the boat. They got approval for this from the captain. After a sumptuous five- course dinner, Mrs Ayinde Ologun also left.

'I wish you a safe and pleasant trip,' were her last words.

Immediately after breakfast the following morning, Dr Jungu called on Mr Hill, the captain of the *MV Mopti*.

'Good morning Dr Jungu. I am now going to the wharf office of Kintu Shipping Lines to telephone our general manager about your dog. Would you like to come with me?'

'Of course! That's why I am here,' he replied impatiently.

Off they went, and after twenty minutes Mr Hill had obtained clearance to carry Shole on the boat. The dog was released and reunited with the Jungus. The children were

21

particularly excited at seeing Shole again. They ran to Captain Hill and shouted:

'Thanks for keeping your word.'

Thereafter they decided to keep Shole out of view in one of their rooms to prevent any intruder from asking further questions about her.

The *MV Mopti* did not sail until six o'clock that evening as a consignment of rubber meant for the United Kingdom arrived late. It was a solid four-day non-stop journey to Buktu, the capital of Kato. The Jungus had a most restful and pleasant period. They played table tennis and tenniquot most of the time. Mr. Hill was particularly friendly to them. He invited them to the bridge of the ship where he explained the ship's operations and navigation system to them. It was exciting and educative. Bunmi was so impressed that he expressed the wish to become a ship's captain in the future. His parents patted him on the back, although they were sure that he did not mean it. They thought his wish was the usual young boy's fantasy. The purser of the *MV Mopti*, Mr Daly, challenged Dr Jungu to a table-tennis match. Mr Daly, the ship's champion for upwards of five years and apparently a flamboyant young Englishman, approached him:

'Doc. I understand you are good at table tennis?'

'I am not an outstanding player by any standard,' was his reply.

'It's going to be Britain versus Africa. It's also winner takes all,' boasted Mr Daly.

'What makes you sound so confident of victory? Is it my looks or my cumbersome African outfit?'

'Surely, you don't look fit with that potbelly of yours,' observed Mr Daly.

'Take a close look at me, mister. Looks could be deceptive.

22

I have not held a bat in three years, but with adequate **warming** up, I promise you a good game.'

Stepping back, Mr Daly took another look at Dr **Jungu** and said rather fiercely:

'If you win, which I doubt, I promise to pay a fine of a dozen cans of beer. In addition, you may become the next custodian of the championship mug of the *MV Mopti*. If, however, you lose, which I am sure you will, you will pay with a dozen cans of the best brewed beer on board.' Waving his bat, he did not forget to add, 'I hope to keep my title come what may.'

Dr Jungu gladly accepted the challenge. He removed the voluminous topmost component of his three-piece African dress and went for his bat, which he carried with him wherever he went. The stage was set for a championship. Although Dr Jungu had no data to go by for a true assessment of Mr Daly's ability, he was convinced that Mr Daly could not be an agile player because of his rotund figure.

The spectators were few. They consisted of the other members of the Jungu family and two sailors, who later proved to be Mr Daly's fanatical supporters. The two contestants sized each other up, while Mr Daly, a brash young man, kept up his verbal offensive shouting:

'I will lick you two-nil in the best of three games. You won't reach ten in either game.'

His two sailor friends roared approval of his stand but failed to **reckon** with Onaola's ability. After only two minutes, the **taller** of the two sailors held the Ping-Pong ball as it flew in his direction from an inaccurate blinder from Mr Daly.

'**You** have had enough of warming up. The weather is fine and **warm**. I am a self-appointed umpire. You must start, head or tail,' he yelled as he tossed up a coin.

'Head and I serve,' replied Mr Daly promptly as he paced up and down by the side of the table.

Mr Daly won the toss and elected to serve. Things worked out the way Dr Jungu wished. The game was only three minutes old when it was over. Dr Jungu had won easily by a score of twenty one to seven. One of the two sailors teased Mr Daly:

'You must be a poor champ. You can only bark but not bite. You even failed to reach ten against a man who had not even touched a bat in the last three years.'

Mr Daly snapped back: 'There is always another chance for a good player. Remember, chums, it takes me a full game to achieve peak performance. It's going to be my turn to laugh and keep Dr Jungu under six. Don't forget that he who laughs last, laughs best. Dr Jungu may yet cry. I volunteer my lunch if I fail to keep my promise.'

The two players changed positions and started another game.

Realizing that Mr Daly was no match for him in the first game, Dr Jungu took it easy and disposed of a now quiet and subdued opponent by a score of twenty-one to thirteen, this time in exactly seventeen minutes. Mr Daly rushed at Dr Jungu at the final count, hugged him and shouted:

'You are great. You are the first person on board the *MV Mopti* ever to beat me so badly. My performance was shocking. You are a much better player than I had anticipated. You have won three things instead of two, twelve cans of beer, the championship mug, and, of course, my lunch.'

Before Dr Jungu could say a word in reply, Mr Daly broke loose and disappeared into his cabin. He re-emerged in about ten minutes before it could be reasonably suspected that he must have run away. He returned with twelve cans of cold beer, which he handed to Dr Jungu with a bow. With the assistance of the other two sailors, Dr Jungu was proclaimed the new table-tennis champion of the *MV Mopti* and was presented with the brightly decorated championship mug amid cheers. The onlooking sailors had expected him to celebrate his easy victory by opening one of the cans of beer and drinking some of it from the championship mug in the traditional way. The taller of the two sailors, whose name Dr Jungu did not bother to find out, said:

'Man, do you want to walk away with the prizes? We are here to celebrate with you. We deserve at least two cans of beer each for our part in cheering you to victory. We also expect you to drink some of this beer from the championship mug. You will not be an exception to our way of life.'

Dr Jungu thanked Mr Daly for keeping his promise and asked to be relieved of the burden of having to eat two lunches. He also thanked him for his sportsmanship. He declared him a good and worthy loser. To the two sailors, he requested that he should be allowed to pour some Coca-Cola into the championship mug, as he was a teetotaler.

"That's great,' replied Mr Bright, the second sailor, who was contributing to the exchange of views for the first time. 'Does it mean that you will pass all the beer to us? We will welcome that, and I assure that you we shall do justice to the beer within the next thirty minutes. Mind you, we will have the empty cans to show as exhibits. I'll be back with twenty-four bottles of ice-cold Coca-Cola in another minute.'

He was soon back with a crate of Coca-Cola. Dr Jungu accepted it in exchange for the beer. He filled the championship mug and raised it high for the championship toast.

'Wait a minute, let us fill our glasses,' requested Mr Bright. Dr Jungu opened three cans of beer one each for the three sailors, and a bottle of Coca-Cola for each member of his family.

'Cheers to the new champ of the *MV Mopti*, long may he reign,' toasted Mr Daly.

The drinking continued until the three sailors had consumed the twelve cans of beer. Dr Jungu and his family then took leave of them and retired to their rooms.

At dawn on the fourth day at sea, Olu tapped at the door of his parent's cabin and, on entering, announced that he had sighted what appeared to him to be land. The Jungus drew the curtain of their room window to one side and saw bright lights here and there in the distance. They were the streetlights of Buktu, the capital city and chief port of the Democratic Republic of Kato. The *MV Mopti* had anchored at sea a little after two o'clock in the morning and was waiting to be piloted into the harbour. However, the signal for the *MV Mopti* to sail to the port was not given until a little after ten o'clock that day. A tug named *Totofioko* approached the ship and, after necessary formalities had been completed; it towed the *MV Mopti* to the quay. Only a few people were at the port. It would have been different had the *MV Mopti* been a passenger boat. The boat anchored precisely twenty minutes past eleven o'clock. After Dr Jungu and his family had completed immigration formalities, they made straight for the arrival hall. Shole was put in a cage, which was carried by a truck-pusher. They anxiously waited till one o'clock for their luggage. Two men, who turned out to be the local representatives of Serti University approached them and asked whether he was the new Professor of Horticulture who had just arrived from Eko. Dr Jungu confirmed this and appeared most pleased to meet the two men, especially as he was becoming apprehensive that he and his family might be stranded. Mr Wiah introduced himself as the liaison officer of the university and presented Mr Chinaga as his assistant. Dr Jungu thereafter presented

26

the members of his family to the two gentlemen, starting with his wife Aida. After exchanging greetings, Mr Wiah, realizing that the Port Authority officials were away on lunch break, extended an invitation to lunch to the Jungu family.

Returning to the port around three o'clock, an official of the health department informed the Jungus that their dog would not be allowed to travel out of Buktu to Serti unless she was seen by a veterinary doctor and certified free of communicable diseases.

'Look, Olu, they want to cause Shole more inconveniences,' observed Bunmi.

'It's high time they left this dog alone.'

'Don't you worry, boys; we are only doing our duty.'

'But, sir, please release our dog to us. We assure you it is not sick.'

Mr Wiah pleaded on behalf of Dr Jungu that the dog be released and that the certification could be easily arranged with a veterinary doctor of Serti University. After twenty minutes of heated exchanges, a senior official of the ministry of health ruled in Mr Wiah's favour, granting the release of the dog, but demanded a written undertaking from Mr Wiah that the certificate would be forwarded to the ministry of health within fifteen days. Shole won her freedom once again.

The customs officials opened every piece of the Jungus' luggage. They searched through most of the contents, and finding nothing incriminating, they released them to Dr Jungu. A lorry was loaded, while a comfortable, long- wheel-base Landrover was provided for the family. They drove out of Buktu a little before it was dark.

3

ARRIVAL AT SERTI

As the Landrover sped toward Serti, one could hear the clatter of the heavy raindrops on its roof. The driver, Ayinla was full of jokes in an attempt to keep everyone awake. He knew the road so well. He raced like a rocket heading for the moon on the straights, but slowed down as he approached the dangerous bends, of which there were very many. The brakes screeched occasionally and Ayinla was prompt in his apologies.

'Sorry, madam, we can't help this once in a while. We shall arrive in Serti safely,' he assured.

Olu and Bunmi recited many nursery rhymes and sang loudly, to the admiration of everyone. They were fully awake and held tight to their pet, Shole.

'Madam, your boys are sharp. At their age they already know so much. The white man is doing wonders with education,' remarked Ayinla.

'Thank you for your kind words, Mr Ayinla,' replied Mrs Jungu.

After over an hour of travelling, the children decided to give the dog some freedom of movement in the Landrover. This was a most unfortunate miscalculation. Shole roamed about in the back compartment of the Landrover like someone

28

stretching his legs. The vehicle suddenly hit a bumpy portion of the road and all of its occupants appeared to have been launched momentarily into space. The dog must have been by an open side window at the time of the impact. Out she went amidst screams of sympathy from the children.

'Mr Ayinla, please stop. Shole is missing,' shouted Olu and Bunmi together.

Ayinla, aware that something serious had occurred, brought the vehicle to a halt some two hundred metres later. It was dark and he found it difficult to reverse his vehicle, which had no back lights. Dr Jungu jumped out and directed Ayinla. To the delight of Ayinla, the children chanted:

'Back up, back up, back up. . .' Shole could not be found on the well-paved road. A thorough search of the unkempt tall grass by the roadside showed that she was surely injured. The dog stood motionless with her glassy eyes wide open. She was dazed. Before picking her up, an examination revealed two deep gashes, one on the forehead and the other by the side of her left ear. Blood streamed out profusely from both wounds. Although afraid that she might attack him, Dr Jungu lifted her carefully to avoid causing more pain. The children became distressed and started to sob in sympathy. Bunmi queried Ayinla as to why he was driving so recklessly and wondered why he failed to slow down at the bump.

'Man must make mistake,' explained Ayinla, 'I could not have seen that particular bump since it was dark. I am also trying to get you to Serti fairly quickly as you must be hungry. That must be your dog's poor luck though, or why could you not hold tight to her as you had done since we left Buktu?'

Meanwhile, more room was created in the Landrover for Shole in the middle row of seats as Bunmi joined his mother on the front seat. Ayinla was instructed to drive more carefully

29

and slowly thereafter, especially so that the bumpy road might not aggravate the dog's pains.

Suddenly there was a big whoop. The dog had vomited. The foul odour rent the air. It was strong and unbearable, but the driver was advised to move on. Twice the Landrover pulled to a stop to allow Dr Jungu to take another close look at Shole. She was still alive, but her pain grew worse.

At five minutes past ten o'clock, they arrived in front of the house of Mr Biliki, the university utilities officer, who took the Jungus to the house allocated to them. It was a simply designed four-bedroom bungalow with a covered verandah, a garage and a large unkempt garden. Dr Jungu informed Mr Biliki of their dog's accident and wondered whether one of the university veterinary doctors could treat her. The Landrover disappeared at top speed into the darkness, Ayinla having been instructed by Mr Biliki to seek the assistance of Dr Jack, the only veterinarian on the campus.

Meanwhile, some old clothes were carefully spread out in a paper carton to serve as a resting place for the dog. Diluted milk was served and she gulped her first drink since morning. A little later, she walked away from the bowl of milk and drooped her head. Bunmi called everyone's attention to the fact that all the milk that the dog had lapped from the bowl was being regurgitated. She vomited profusely as if the milk had irritated her throat. Dr Jungu moved near her to offer some help, but the stench of the regurgitated milk kept the others at a distance. The dog was next offered some cold water, but this she also rejected.

It was now obvious that she would not be able to hold any liquid and perhaps any food. Everyone became apprehensive over the seriousness of the injuries she must have sustained. However, they were unable to determine the extent of internal injuries. The driver returned with the information that Dr Jack was away in Buktu and that he was expected back at Serti the following evening.

Dr Jungu was outraged by the fact that Dr Jack was the only veterinary doctor in the university town of Serti. He stared at the ceiling in deep thought and disbelief. The fact suddenly began to dawn on him that Kato must indeed be short of qualified, high-grade manpower at various levels. He could not but think that the dog's luck had run out. It was ironic that such ill luck should befall her at the journey's end and at a place where he had assumed that many veterinary doctors would be on post and readily available. He doubted that the dog would survive this ordeal to wag her tail in appreciation of the strenuous efforts everyone had made to keep her alive. Poor dog, she could still be seen pacing up and down slowly, but unhappily and painfully along the verandah. She was mute. She could not even wag her tail or bark. Realizing that it was late, everyone went to bed, leaving the dog to her fate.

The children were up earlier than usual. They must have had a bad night. Thoughts of Shole's condition wrote deep sorrow on their faces. Aida found them by the verandah as if they had kept a vigil all night. Bunmi remarked that the levels of the milk and water in the two bowls placed at the verandah had remained the same, which pointed to the fact that the dog had realized it was no use trying to lap up any more liquid. The children scrubbed the verandah with water to which some dettol had been added in an effort to remove the foul odour of the vomited milk. She stared at the food, surely feeling like tasting a little of it. She walked away from the bowl of food, again drooping her head. Aida could not bear it anymore. It was beginning to seem as if her own child had fallen seriously sick.

31

Thoughts of Shole's loyalty and effectiveness as a watch-dog flashed through her mind. She recalled that the dog was given to their family six years ago by a departing English colleague of her husband. Shole was in fact older than Olu, Aida's younger son. She struck fear into the hearts of visitors to the residence of the Jungus - friends and foes alike. Aida remembered how the dog used to bark at anything that moved near their house. The family felt perfectly safe with her around them.

Shole had three beautiful male puppies a year after coming to live with the Jungus. A female teacher friend of the family living about half a kilometre away was so impressed by her efficiency as a watchdog that she begged for one of the puppies. The smallest puppy was given away. Aida recalled the children had taken special interest in Shole's puppies and were unhappy that one of them had been given away. When they got wind of the fact that the teacher had taken one of the puppies, they made straight for her house and demanded that the puppy be returned to them forthwith.

'We want our puppy back. Give us our puppy ....' cried the children. The teacher at first took the request as a joke, only to have the children engaged in a weeping session. As they wept, they chanted: 'Give us our dog,' as if the teacher had stolen it.

The teacher became embarrassed. As far as the children were concerned, she had failed to clarify the position satisfactorily. She was therefore forced to return the puppy, although reluctantly. Such was the close attachment to Shole and now with her puppies that they had built over the years. Aida remembered how she had had to persuade Olu and Bunmi that the puppy should be given to the teacher as they would not have had Shole in the first instance if another friend had not been so kind and nice to them. It took four weeks of daily lectures and coaxing to convince the children of this.

Shole, it was recalled, was left with her remaining two puppies: a big rather quiet, strong and gluttonous one with glossy black coat later named Jury, and a smaller unruly but beautiful one with a woolly brown coat, fondly called Rolly. Shole was indeed a good mother to Rolly and Jury. She fed them regularly with her own milk. This of course was supplemented lavishly with diluted milk. It was a routine for Olu and Bunmi to serve the puppies this treat every afternoon and evening. They also bathed and towelled them once weekly. Rolly and Jury grew fast and soon achieved twice the size of their mother.

Shole had the intuition that her puppies should be as good watch-dogs as she had been. She taught them by example to bark hard at any approaching person, but never to bite. The puppies derived much pleasure running after a frightened visitor who had had to take to his heels. This was not fun to the unlucky visitor. They caused embarrassing situations a few times when visiting dignitaries had to be rescued after they had succeeded in bringing them to the ground, sometimes wrapped up in their flowing African garments called *agbada*. It was quite a spectacle! Messengers were scared stiff to carry files to the residence of Dr Jungu. Everyone had come to know and respect Shole, Rolly, and Jury.

Every night as soon as it was dark, Shole seemed to post strong, black Jury at that corner of the house facing the approach road, while unruly Rolly was by the kitchen guarding the backyard portion of the house. Shole herself reigned supreme at the main entrance. She lay by the foot mat at the front door. The dogs did not leave these positions until the next morning. They stuck to this arrangement religiously and

33

barked together at any suspected movement after a signal from the dog that first sighted the possible culprit. Such was their efficiency and effectiveness that Dr Jungu cracked a joke that he could afford to sleep soundly and snore. He was very sure a thief would not dare to burgle his residence with the Shole trio around.

The night watchman who was paid to guard the residence of the Jungus also acknowledged the dogs' effectiveness. He seemed most pleased that they had effectively taken over his own duties, but without loss of pay to him. It was obvious that he was taking money under false pretences for a job he did poorly. However, he rewarded Shole and her loyal puppies occasionally with remnants of bush meat, portions of giant rats and soft bones from the meat shop. It was not surprising that the watchman had made it a habit to drop off to sleep even before the children who routinely went to bed around eight in the evening.

It occurred to Aida that this might be the end of an era with the Shole trio since Rolly and Jury were earlier given away to another friend just before the family left Ibadan. Aida wanted help from anywhere if it would save Shole's life. She was indeed very precious to the family and was considered a member of the Jungu family in her own right.

By evening there was a hard tap on the main door of Dr Jungu's home. Aida suspecting that it could be the veterinary surgeon, rushed there and swung open the front door. A chubby, cheerful, middle aged white figure greeted her with the usual courtesies.

'Are you the veterinary surgeon?' inquired Aida politely.

'Yes, Mrs Jungu, I hope that is your name. I returned from Buktu some ten minutes ago only to be informed of the accident that your dog had had. May I have a look at it please?' requested Dr Jack.

Aida led Dr Jack to the verandah where Shole was found doing her usual beat. Her movements were now sluggish. It would appear that the end was near. Dr Jack carried her most tenderly and examined her thoroughly. He detected the two external wounds, which were already healing, but suspected that she must have had very serious internal injuries. He was unable to determine precisely the nature of the internal injuries, but explained that this had caused the dog grievous pain and discomfort. Dr Jack decided that she needed a painkiller. He therefore administered it and promised to come by the next morning to follow up the treatment.

Every attempt to get Shole to eat or drink failed again. Members of the Jungu family went to bed full of concern for the dog's deteriorating condition.

A loud, shrill noise aroused Dr Jungu from his sleep around four o'clock in the morning. As the shrill noise was repeated, he woke Aida up and explained that it must have come from Shole. Naturally, as this was the first time the dog was suspected to have made any noise since the accident occurred two days earlier, it was logical to assume that she was probably improving. To confirm this, Dr Jungu rushed to the kitchen made some fresh diluted milk, and switched on the verandah light. He found Shole lying on the neatly laid old clothes in the paper carton. This was the first time she had used her makeshift bed since it was made. She lay quietly in the paper box as though all was well. He moved nearer, put the bowl of milk stealthily by her side, but did not try to get her to drink. He was convinced that she needed a minimum of disturbance. Assuming that all was well, he returned to Aida, confident that the dog had really improved. He didn't realize that that was Shole's last call. By seven thirty, when the Jungu family went to the table for breakfast, Aida became uneasy.

'Onaola, do you think all is well with that dog?' 'It's rather early to ask such questions. I wish you had got up when I did to feed her.'

Shortly afterward, Aida advised that the family take an early morning stroll. When, during the course of it, Aida noticed that the children had been attracted away by a shrub with pretty, bright-red flowers, she broke the ice by whispering to her husband that Shole had died peacefully in her sleep. He was shocked! He stood motionless for a brief moment.

'You don't mean it! She looked very well earlier on.'

'She probably was dead after that early morning noise. It must have been her last noise,' added Aida. She implored him not to break the sad news to the children for fear that it might upset them.

They both agreed that he should immediately arrange for the removal of Shole's remains to prevent the children from becoming aware of what had happened. Dr Jungu thereafter contacted Dr Jack, who picked up the dog for a post-mortem examination. He announced later:

'By Jove, your dog was indeed strong to have survived for so long. Her bladder was ruptured and nothing could have saved her.'

Poor Shole was given a grand but quiet burial. The children were kept in the dark about what had happened for another month. That was the sad end of a most friendly, loyal dog.

4

INITIATION INTO UNIVERSITY LIFE

It rained hard all night. Flashes of lightning streaked across the sky at regular intervals. These were accompanied by high winds and heavy thunderous bangs which appeared to shake the buildings on the campus to their very foundations. Olu and Bunmi were terribly frightened. They shouted for help as if they were being hounded by Shole's ghost, and sought refuge in the bedroom of their parents.

By morning, the heavy rain had turned into light showers. Dr Jungu had not anticipated this type of continuously rainy weather. He had neither an umbrella nor a raincoat. As he also had no car, he would have to walk to meet the dean of the faculty of forestry and horticulture in his office for briefing. In the end, he decided to stay at home until the situation improved. He wished he had a telephone. At least he would have been able to inform the dean that he might be unable to keep the nine o'clock appointment. Moreover he did not want to give the impression that being on time did not mean much to him. He stood inside the porch of his house expecting a miracle to rescue him from the embarrassing plight.

Like a dream come true, a car soon pulled up by his residence. The driver was a Chinese. He introduced himself as Dr Chien Fu, a senior lecturer in the department of silviculture. He explained that he had seen Dr Jungu at a distance and had suspected that he might need a ride. Dr Jungu gladly accepted the offer and thanked Dr Fu for the kind gesture. Dr Jungu reached the dean's office three minutes before the hour of nine. His arrival was announced to the dean, Professor Nada, by his shapely secretary, Miss Otit. As the door to the dean's office swung wide open, he was greeted warmly by Professor Nada. He shook Dr Jungu's hands so firmly and repeatedly, a typical Kato way of welcome, that the latter's fingers were almost crushed under the severe pressure.

'Surprised you made it on time. It's by and large African time we are used to on this campus,' remarked Professor Nada cynically. 'You are here for a briefing session, but first let me inform you of an important administrative change being contemplated.'

'By whom?' asked Dr Jungu.

'That's unimportant, but I think it is in your own interest not to accept the headship of the department of horticulture. I have had to change the head of that department thrice in as many years. First, I had an American who was extremely lazy.'

'That's most unusual,' cut in Dr Jungu in disbelief his mouth was agape.

'I later had a hard-working, intelligent, and brilliant man from Nigeria who could not get on well with the Kato people. His only crime was that he required efficiency and hard work from everyone in the department. I must warn you, Kato people are lazy, wish to head every department, but refuse to shoulder responsibility or co-operate with outsiders heading departments. Finally, I had another good African who was a total failure as an administrator although he proved an excellent research scientist.'

'You must have a curious lot of Kato people in the horticul-

38

ture department. How many are they if I may ask- twenty, thirty.. ?'

'Just a handful, only eight, but the department has eleven members on its staff,' replied Professor Nada. 'I have a clue, an excellent idea, I suppose. I have invited an old Professor, some sixty years old, from America to head the department. He is a crafty old fox. This will prevent unnecessary friction amongst you Africans,' concluded Professor Nada sarcastically.

'For God's sake, when did you white folks start to equate old age with wisdom? Are you suggesting that I should be just Professor of horticulture and not head of the department as well?' queried a surprised Dr Jungu.

'Precisely,' replied Professor Nada with a nauseating grin.

'But I am not convinced by your arguments, especially as I have successfully co-ordinated the research efforts of over thirty-five highly qualified scientists in Nigeria in the last four years. Handling just eleven scientists, or is it lecturers you call them, should be a lot easier. Do you think you will carry the president of the university on this, as it might set aside an earlier decision of the Appointments and Promotions Committee?'

'Leave that to me. I will take care of things and tie the loose ends,' retorted a most pleased Professor Nada, feeling that Dr Jungu was now sold on his idea.

Dr Jungu reasoned to himself that the dean was in no position to affect his status. He had considered it a waste of valuable time engaging in further exchanges on such a trivial matter. He reasoned, however, that if the dean were successful in his plot, his consolation lay in the fact that he would have to devote his entire time to research and teaching and that all the administrative headaches would be inherited by the so-called wise old American.

Professor Nada, sensing that Dr Jungu had recovered from his bewilderment, continued the briefing.

'There are seven departments in the faculty of forestry and horticulture: silviculture; wood technology; forest pathology; soils; tree improvement, and forest botany all being different specialties of forestry and of course, horticulture. The department of horticulture deals with the production of fruits, vegetables and flowers. Our emphasis naturally is on the first two items.'

Two hard knocks were heard on the door.

'Yes, come in,' said Dean Nada.

'Good morning sir, may I interrupt you for a moment?' asked Dr Carpenter.

'Oh, let me introduce you to Dr Jungu, our new Professor of horticulture.'

Drs Carpenter and Jungu moved toward each other and exchanged greetings.

'Nice to meet you,' they said to each other.

'I hope you don't mind if I attend to Dr Carpenter. It won't be a minute,' said Dean Nada to Dr Jungu.

'That's all right; I can wait.'

Turning to Dr Carpenter, Dean Nada asked:

'Now what can I do for you?'

'I need to recruit two labourers immediately for harvesting some vegetables, sir. Army worms have descended on my experimental plot and you know, sir, what damage they can do in a short time. Prompt harvesting will at least bring in some revenue.'

'Is that all? Simple. You have my permission to hire the labourers.'

'Immense thanks, sir.'

'Well, Dr Jungu, I have to approve every penny spent here.

Unless this is done, Kato people often abuse their office. Mind you, I am acting as the head of your department until a substantive head is appointed,' stated Dean Nada.

'Is this how departments are run here? You mean I have to run to my head of department before I can hire labourers?'

'I wish you will take a cue from Dr Carpenter. He was indeed respectful when addressing me. I must warn that I demand an occasional 'sir' from you too.'

'Me?'

'It is just an advice. Maybe I should take you round the faculty to introduce you to your colleagues, starting of course with those in the horticulture department.'

'I see. I hope Professors are also colleagues too, even when some are serving as deans,' replied Dr Jungu, smiling.

'I mean every bit of what I have just said. It's not a joke.'

Professors Nada and Jungu walked briskly to the dean's saloon car, parked under a mango tree near his office. They drove to one end of the campus to see the vegetable farm. It was a small, nonexperimental five-acre plot.

'Is this the university farm?' asked Dr Jungu.

Stammering, Professor Nada said:

'Yes. You see, there is actually no university farm. It is a million-dollar question you asked. This type of question is posed year after year even by visitors to our campus. Not much is being done here by way of research. Funds are limited. As we move along, I will show you the other two experimental farms. We hope the situation will improve fairly soon. See those grubs! I presume this must be Dr Carpenter's plot.'

'You mean that you are not even sure it is?'

'Well, there isn't much time for visiting the plots. It's an uphill task administering this faculty.'

Surprised that Dean Nada spent most of his time in his

41

air-conditioned office, he decided not to ask any more questions to save him from further embarrassment. After examining the other two plots, Dr Jungu expressed disappointment at what he had seen. He reasoned that a lot more could have been achieved if a concerted effort had been made to start an experimental farm some ten years earlier, when the young university was born. It was also obvious that most lecturers and professors at Serti University were not contributing much to knowledge through research. He felt they were 'classroom dons.'

The next stop was at the office of Mr Lambe, senior lecturer in floriculture.

'Mr Lambe, meet Dr Jungu, our new Professor of horticulture who arrived just three days ago.'

'Nice to meet you. I hope you had a pleasant trip to Serti,' asked Mr Lambe, offering his hand of friendship to Dr Jungu. Mr Lambe, apparently venting his resentment, continued: 'Had the university authorities advertised this job in Kato, I would have applied. It appears a prophet has no honour in his country.'

Jungu was terribly shocked and embarrassed by the unwarranted and inappropriate comments of Mr Lambe. Although he was tempted to believe that, like the old colonial administrators, Professor Nada must have survived at Serti on his policy of divide and rule, the envy demonstrated by Mr Lambe, 'a son of the soil,' was sufficient to make an unsuspecting new-comer to Serti justify some of Professor Nada's actions. Unpleasant experiences with other Serti lecturers, however, soon lent support to some of Professor Nada's generalizations. As in any country, Dr Jungu detected that there were some conscientious as well as many lazy lecturers amongst the Kato people on the staff of the university, but that the citizens of Kato through their actions and behaviour probably played into Dean Nada's hands.

It took two and a half hours to complete the rounds. By then, a few things had become obvious to Dr Jungu. He had for instance discovered that every head of department on the faculty was white and American. He argued with himself whether this was deliberate. He noted that except for one distinguished American Professor whose achievements were substantial but who had passed his peak, many of the so-called experts and heads of departments exhibited mediocrity and should not have been appointed to such high university offices. Regrettably, they had neither the qualifications nor the cognate experience to justify their appointments to the enviable positions in which they found themselves. Like manna from heaven, the positions would appear to have fallen on their laps.

Dr Jungu further observed that Professor Nada must have used naked power to impose on the staff Mr Campbell, a young, inexperienced American in his twenties, as acting head of the department of wood technology. This young man had obtained his B.Sc. in wood technology three years earlier and a master's degree the following year. Before coming to Serti, he had had no university teaching experience. Dr Jungu began to feel that Professor Nada must be a dubious character with a perverted sense of justice and someone who rejoiced in applying a double standard to whites and blacks. Otherwise, why was he so keen to have another white American, not necessarily more reputable than himself, as head of the department of horticulture? Dr Jungu had three degrees, and a specialty in post-harvest physiology. In addition, he had ten years' post-doctorate experience. He had published several outstanding papers on his research in Nigeria in reputable scientific journals and had held responsible research administrative positions for upward of four years. He considered his contributions to agricultural knowledge more appropriate in this setting. Moreover, he had taught horticulture to the degree students at the University of Western Nigeria for six years. Jungu felt that he was more eminently qualified to head a department and wished the president of the university would not act unilaterally by setting aside the earlier decision of the Appointments and Promotions Committee.

'You must feel happy returning to this refreshing, cool environment,' noted Dean Nada as the two men returned to his air-conditioned office.

'It surely feels good here. I hope I will be fortunate to have such a nice office, at least one which is air-conditioned.'

'Ah-ha. Only deans and heads of departments qualify for air-conditioned offices.'

'Now you see why I should not give up the headship of the horticulture department.'

'But I thought you Africans are already used to this heat.'

Dr Jungu opened his mouth wide in amazement. He restrained himself to avoid another unpleasant exchange. He was a new man at Serti. He did not want the impression created that he was cantankerous. He felt that he needed to know a little more about Dean Nada's background to be able to predict his attitude toward members of the faculty, especially the black ones. He decided to be a pretender for once. He merely laughed at Dean Nada's comment, saying.

'You know, it was a bit cool out there in the field. It was only about twenty-nine degrees centigrade. At this time of the year in Nigeria, temperatures rise to thirty-one or even thirty-three degrees centigrade.'

'There you are, I knew I was right.'

Unannounced, Mr Campbell, the young acting head of the department of wood technology walked into the dean's office. Without an atom of courtesy, he made straight for Dean Nada:

44

'Say, I have a few problems up my sleeve.'

'Dr Jungu, I hope you will excuse us for one minute. I hate discussing departmental matters in the presence of people not in that particular department,' explained Dean Nada.

'Don't you think I should go away and return tomorrow to continue the briefing? I hate being in your way. I don't want to appear to be a cog in the wheel of the faculty progress.'

'No no. In five minutes I'll call you in.'

Dr Jungu walked out and started to pace up and down the corridor of the dean's office. He was most displeased at the treatment meted out to him. Sensing what must have happened, the chief clerk, Mr Amodu, offered him a chair and remarked in a feeble voice:

'That's what Africans suffer here. Isn't it a shame that you had to be asked to go out for that white boy?'

'So you know what has just happened?'

'African staff suffer such indignities here everyday sir.'

'But why is that so?'

'These white boys are lords in this place, sir. They run us around and treat everyone like a dog. They don't even respect my gray hairs - a symbol of old age.'

'You mean no one ever resents such treatment?'

'Brother, this is the Democratic Republic of Kato. The Kato man is his own enemy. People like Dr Carpenter are the 'good boys' of these whites. They spy for them and gossip to them. Be careful, sir, not to associate closely with such people. I need to brief you adequately about these white boys and. . .'

Pa Amodu was forced to swallow the last part of that sentence. Both Mr Campbell and the dean had suddenly appeared at the corridor. Although Dean Nada was unable to put together exactly what had transpired between Dr Jungu

45

and Pa Amodu, he suspected that the old man might be attempting to make friends with Dr Jungu.

'Amodu, come into my office.'

'Yes, sir. I'll be right there.'

On entering he scolded him for being so intimate with Dr Jungu.

'I hope you have not been letting our secrets out to the new Professor.'

'No, sir.'

'Then, why did you two appear to be engaged in very friendly exchanges?'

'You can trust me, sir. My loyalty is first to you and our American friends. Dr Jungu only asked me about the market and where he can get certain food items like okro, yam, 'gari,' 'egusi,' et cetera.'

'You are still the good old fox that I thought you were. Now listen. You have to keep an eye on Dr Jungu. He appears arrogant and disrespectful. Unlike you good guys, he won't even say 'sir' to me. He is the first of his kind here. He may turn out to be a bad influence.'

'You know, he even appeared annoyed when you sent him out for Mr Campbell. I made friendly approaches so that I could know how he really felt.'

'Good old Amodu. We need more of you here. How is madam today?'

'Fine, sir, but she has some fever.'

'I am awfully sorry to hear that. Take this ten dollars and buy some medicine for her. I wish her a quick recovery.'

'Thank you, sir. Madam will surely come to thank you in the house when she is well.'

Pa Amodu returned to his room feeling convinced that Dean Nada had misplaced his confidence. He was a veteran of

46

many wars fought on behalf of imperial powers and yet he only achieved the rank of sergeant-major. He had a good educational background for a man of his time. After obtaining the old standard six certificate, he attended the much-talked-of Crown Prince Grammar School. He was a little above average in performance but he spoke the Queen's English. Throughout his stay in the school, he also wrote English essays, which were reputed to be easily the best. His luck ran out after only three years in the grammar school when his father suddenly died during one of the ever-present smallpox epidemics. Pa Amodu was forced to quit school and fend for himself to keep body and soul together. The going was rough for him all the way. At first, he had thought of becoming a mechanic, but gave up this idea after two and a half months' trial since apprentice mechanics were not paid any wages in those days. It was then that he decided to join the army. He served loyally for twelve years before obtaining an honourable discharge. He saw action during the second world war in Burma. He thereafter elected to join the department of education as a third-class clerk. From there, he was seconded to Serti University at its inception. He had been there ever since. Pa Amodu was indeed a self-made man who had gone through the mill. He knew what suffering could be at the hands of the white man. He admired Dr Jungu for his courage. He was convinced Dr Jungu needed support and help. He had resolved to help him, even if he had to pretend to be a 'good boy' to the dean.

Pa Amodu lifted the telephone receiver.

'Hello, hello,' he said.

'It's Dean Nada here,' replied the voice on the other end.

'Hello, sir, I am sorry, sir, I did not know it was you.'

'That's all right, I know you thought it was one of those African staff members.'

'I am sorry, sir.'

'It's OK. Is Dr Jungu still around?'

'Yes, sir.'

'Call him to speak on the telephone.'

'Please Dr Jungu, come and take this call. It is from the dean,' said Amodu, trembling.

'Hello, Jungu speaking.'

'I am afraid you will have to see me this afternoon at three o'clock. I am expecting some visitors this morning at eleven o'clock and I will need to take them to lunch.'

'That's all right. See you then.'

On dropping the telephone receiver, Dr Jungu asked Pa Amodu whether he could see him outside for a minute. Pa Amodu agreed. They moved to the open field in front of the dean's office, and immediately Pa Amodu started to point here and there as if he was trying to show Dr Jungu the different places on campus. This was contrived to deceive Dean Nada, who might be spying at them with his binoculars from his office.

'Pa Amodu, I need your assistance to survive here,' appealed Dr Jungu.

'Please count on my loyalty, sir.'

'Can you come to my office during lunch break for a chat?'

'That is a dangerous proposition, sir. The dean has his good boys everywhere. They might report me and that will affect my progress, sir.'

'How then can we meet?'

'Nothing is impossible, sir. Why not in your house?'

'That's a good idea. What about having lunch with me?'

'Thank you, sir, for the kind invitation. That's not a bad idea.'

'But how will you get there unnoticed?'

48

'Do you know my age, sir? I am close to sixty. I should have retired three years ago, but my 'official' age is only forty-nine. These white boys cannot fool me. Africa belongs to us, not them. Leave your kitchen door open, sir. I will come in with some vegetables as if someone had sent me to deliver them to you, sir.'

'Please have five dollars for any purchases that you might undertake on my behalf.'

'Thank you, sir. Let me return to the office before the dean starts to ask for me.'

'Thank you and goodbye for now. Don't fail to turn up at one o'clock.'

Dr Jungu got home around twelve noon and reported his experiences to his wife. Aida was convinced that Dean Nada and his clique did not want Africans on equal terms. She felt Serti was not likely to have them for long.

'Onaola the sooner we get out of here the better.'

'Young lady, take heart. It's not all that gloomy.'

'Remember you told everyone in Nigeria that you intended to be here for five years. I will be surprised if you last one year. I suppose they either push you out or . . .'

'Or what? Just look around, you won't see one Kato man of equal status with us. These white folks are bound to treat all blacks alike irrespective of their status. I am however confident that as time goes on, many of them, including the pompous Nada will learn to treat us with respect.'

'Some of them have fixed ideas about us, you know. Remember your experiences as a student in America?'

'Aida, you never seem to forget those unpleasant experiences. Surely these white folks make black people feel cursed. It's not their fault. I still maintain that the ones here will change.'

'Mr Optimist! It's going to be an uphill task in an environment where people like Dr Carpenter descend so low as to lick Nada's boots. You may have to conform to succeed.'

'Me? Conform? Never! Aida, I thought by now you should have realized that I don't compromise on principles.'

'That's why some of your friends say you lack diplomacy. Can't you pretend and give Nada a false sense of confidence? It could pay off in the long run.'

'I will think about that. By the way, Pa Amodu is coming to join us for lunch. He should be here in another twenty minutes.'

'And who is he? A new friend?'

'Aida, he is the chief clerk in the dean's office. He was most sympathetic to me today. We can learn a lot about the dean from him.'

'Beware; Pa Amodu may be one of those in the pay of the dean to spy on you. He could also exploit his association with you to suck you dry.'

'Aida, don't you even feel I can cope with such situations? Pa Amodu looks a genuine friend.'

'But what can Pa Amodu know about Dean Nada?'

'You underrate these clerks and messengers. They carry all the files–secret, confidential and all. They also dispatch all the letters. Certainly they take advantage of the situation to read all-important documents. Pa Amodu must have seen everyone's curriculum vitae.'

'You have a point there. What can I get ready for you both in only fifteen minutes?'

'Some rice and baked beans should be all right.'

Aida disappeared into the kitchen, washed the rice and put it on the fire. Meanwhile he went for Olu and Bunmi who had just started to attend a school one kilometre away from their house.

'Mummy, Mummy, we are back from school.'

'My dear, how was it?'

50

'Not bad. We made new friends–Nancy and Dorothy Nada and Kulumbu and Tahir, the sons of the president of the university, Dr Oranlola.'

'How about that? You children are surely making it here,' remarked their father.

'Go and change out of your uniforms and get ready for lunch. We are expecting Pa Amodu to join us soon,' added Aida.

'Ok.'

It was a quarter past one and yet Pa Amodu was not in sight. The Jungus were in doubt as to whether he would still come. The children were getting impatient and hungry. Aida advised them to go and wash their hands and come to the table. Suddenly a noise came from the kitchen door, as if someone was trying to force it open. Dr Jungu ran there, turned the key, and Pa Amodu sneaked in.

'I am almost on time,' he said, as they moved toward the living room.

Hm! We were just about to give you up. Meet my wife Aida. This is Pa Amodu.'

'Pleased to meet you, madam.'

'May we go straight to the table,' invited Aida.

Everyone ate well and Pa Amodu asked for a second helping. He thanked Mrs Jungu for a most delicious meal, adding jokingly that he would surely pay another visit before long.

'You will be most welcome. Please make this your second home,' said Aida.

'And no formalities, either. Just walk in,' added Dr Jungu.

They retired to the study. Pa Amodu thanked them again for being so nice to him. He told them it was good he had this opportunity so soon after their arrival at Serti to say a few things about Dean Nada to guide them in their dealings with him.

51

'Dean Nada was born forty-two years ago on a small island in the South Pacific. He grew up in an environment where he had never seen a black man until he visited America some six years ago. He had a good basic education and possessed a B.Sc. degree in engineering and a doctorate degree in wood utilization. He had worked for eight years as a research officer in his country before joining an international organization as the project manager of a wood technology team in South America. He is used to giving instructions unchallenged as he had always worked with people of much lower rank than his. All his three years plus here, he has failed to realize that he is working among equals. The Americans sent him here as one of the experts to aid our faculty of forestry.'

'Since he is not an American how come he is the dean?' asked Dr Jungu.

'He is not the most powerful person in the group, sir. He himself is told what to do by the team director. It used to be a Dr Whitehead.'

'But why is Dean Nada not the head of the wood technology department in view of his qualifications, experience, and seniority?'

'Ah-ha! These yankees are clever, sir. They want to control every department in the faculty. That's why Nada is dean and they brought in young, inexperienced Campbell as acting head since it is an unwritten understanding that a dean should not head any department, sir.'

'Pa Amodu, do you in all honesty think I can get on with Dean Nada?'

'That's a tricky question, sir. As for me, I will say 'yes, sir' to him in reply to any questions from him. You are supposed to be his equal, but I don't think he would want anything short of servility.'

'Impossible! I just cannot do that!'

'My advice to you, sir, is that you should not mind pretending to be foolish to succeed. You may have to stoop to conquer. I must leave you now, sir. It's ten minutes to two o'clock.'

'You have been most helpful. I hope it won't be too long before you come again. Goodbye for now.'

'Bye-bye for now, sir.'

'Why these formalities, Pa Amodu? I hate to see a man as old as my father punctuating every reply to me with 'sir.' I bet you know I am yet to receive an accolade from the Queen.'

'That's how the white man brought us up, sir, to respect and worship those in authority.'

'From now on, call me Onaola if you please, and no more 'sir.' OK?'

'Goodbye and good day,' greeted Pa Amodu.

Dr Jungu returned to the dean's office a few minutes before three o'clock. He was announced to the dean, who asked him in.

'With our visit to all departments still so fresh in your mind, I suppose you have a few questions,' Professor Nada stated.

'None for now. I would rather wait till the question of the headship of the department of horticulture is resolved,' replied Dr Jungu calmly.

Both men agreed to meet again at three o'clock on the following day in the dean's office.

Dr Jungu had been allocated no office, even though the dean was aware of his intention to arrive in Serti four months earlier. Every other lecturer had an office equipped to some degree. But he was the most senior African ever on the faculty. He was the first full Professor.

An unusual circular was issued around nine o'clock in the morning of Dr Jungu's fourth day at Serti by the Office of the

President of the University. It read simply: 'Professor Blake, a renowned horticulturist from the U.S.A., has been appointed head of the department of horticulture. He arrives in three weeks, but before that time Dean Nada will take charge of the department.'

African lecturers congregated in twos and threes. They all suspected Professor Blake must be white.

The speed with which the new decision was reached and circulated baffled Dr Jungu. He had doubts as to whether the university committees were allowed to function freely and properly. Neither did he realize at that point that Dean Nada was the alternate president of the university. He later discovered that it was more often convenient for President Oranlola to set aside the decisions of university committees and act according to the dictates of his mind. It did not take long to query whether this arrogant man of an administrator-president possessed a sound mind. Other forward-looking members of the academic staff believed that the president must be feathering his own nest. Many others had doubts as to the exact motive of the president, but one thing was sure: he implemented the advice of the white 'experts' and especially that given by Professor Nada.

Dr Jungu cast his mind back on his social experience while a student in the United States. Although he was by far the post-graduate student with the highest cumulative grade-point average in his department, he had been a victim of social prejudice just for being black.

He remembered his encounter with the chairman of his department. He had wanted a vacation job to supplement the monthly allowance from his scholarship in order to assist in paying his wife's way through college. His major Professor had just informed him that he would employ him during the summer, but that he needed the approval of the chairman of the department. This was never granted. This led to a confrontation between young Jungu and the chairman of his department. One or two black American students wondered why he should have raised his voice in protest. Reluctant at first to hit the nail on the head, the chairman advised him to sell his ten-year-old jalopy if he needed money so badly. Of course he countered the argument by explaining that he considered a car, however old, an essential luxury since there was no regular bus service in the university city. Moreover, he had observed that some of the Americans (and they were all white) who enjoyed financial assistance from the department as graduate assistants drove expensive flashy new cars. In addition most of their wives were employed as secretaries in the department. By education, he reasoned that he, who contributed to the university purse either from his tuition or his wife's college fees, deserved help much more than those who only siphoned money out of the college. Thinking that his submission was foolproof, he shuddered when the chairman suggested that he advise his wife to quit college and save the money for their upkeep. He promptly ran down the chairman as an enemy of progress. He felt ashamed that these were the same people deriding Africans as illiterate, ignorant, and backward. He could not understand why such a civilized, well-read man failed to see the need to educate another African woman through self-effort. The chairman closed the issue by announcing to him that he had made up his mind to give the vacation job to a white student.

Dr Jungu remembered standing speechless in disbelief at the attitude of a head of department he had respected up to that moment. He was undecided whether the fear of economic domination or white racism had governed the man's attitude.

One thing was sure; he made up his mind that his wife would remain in college.

Dr Jungu had dreamed of his return to his native Africa, when he would walk the streets with his face in the skies - a proud first-class citizen. This did not come to pass. In Nigeria, people with white skin had the best jobs, were allocated the most comfortable houses, and got the best pay packet. Ironically, many of them needed to be tutored by a lower-paid but more accomplished African before finding their feet. To see the same white man that someone beat in class coming to lord it over him made one feel that the African was either cursed or needed some self-reexamination and soul-searching. He often asked himself: Is this the price that has to be paid for development? The experience at Kato was the same. It began to appear as though second-class citizenry was the preserve of the black man. But who is to blame? Everyone who had failed to have a social rebirth and be rid of the colonial brain-washing. Every black man surely needs debriefing. He felt convinced that it was utter disgrace and failure on the part of the black man to blame the imperialist for his sufferings. With the thought, white you are right, black you are wrong, lingering on his mind, he decided to call it a day.

Four weeks on a campus without an office for a Professor was enough to discourage anyone but Dr Jungu. Professor Blake had arrived. The red carpet was laid for him. He had two offices; one air-conditioned and the other serviced with two electric fans. Two days before Professor Blake arrived, Dr Jungu had been allocated Room 34 in the department of horticulture as his office by the Dean. It was an empty room with broken window-panes. It became a pool when it rained, as water ran in freely through the broken windows. Lizards apparently looking for an abode shared the office space with

56

him. To his surprise, the same Room 34 had been acquired by Professor Blake as his second office. Sensing that there was a conflict, he quickly approached the dean for clarification.

'You now have a head of department, please refer all matters to him henceforth,' stated Dean Nada, sporting his deceptive grin.

In a rage Dr Jungu, drove straight over to Professor Blake who was then in his other office, the airconditioned one located some two kilometres away at the other end of the campus.

'Good morning, Professor Blake. I hate to bother you with trivial matters, but I need an office to function effectively. I understand you are to have Room 34 in the department of horticulture as your second office.'

'It was Dean Nada who assigned Room 34 to me as well. You may have it. I don't really need it. Have the key to Room 34, it's all yours,' assured Professor Blake.

He murmured his thank you and made straight for the door. It appeared there was a strong pull on the door in the opposite direction, so he let it go. In came Dean Nada almost colliding with him. Dean Nada blushed at the sight of Dr Jungu. It turned out that he had rushed to Professor Blake to advise him not to part with Room 34. It was too late. Professor Blake was bound to stand by his promise.

It took six weeks to put the office in shape. A decent table and three chairs were supplied, but he had had to assemble abandoned shelves, an electric fan, and a filing cabinet from here and there. It soon became obvious to everyone that Dr Jungu would have to fight for everything in Kato to succeed. His plan was to stay in Serti for five years. He felt this would be a positive way to contribute his share to the development of a young African university.

5

JUNGU FINDS HIS FEET

Nigerians numbered close to thirty on the staff of the university. They came from different ethnic groups, but experience had shown that, when abroad, Nigerians tended to forget their ethnic differences lest they suffer and sink together in the ocean of uncertainty. They represented a closely-knit clan -- a happy, friendly group. It was not a strange place after all for the Jungus. Traditionally, the oldest senior Nigerian, one of the academic staff gave a party at the beginning of each session to acquaint the new arrivals with those who had come before them. What an occasion for feasting and merry-making! Every Nigerian at Serti looked forward to it. It was like an annual pilgrimage to the holy land. Elder Babajo never allowed the day to pass without tendering advice to the new-comers. His annual thesis revolving around survival at Serti sounded like this:

'This is not your country, although you are as black as the average Kato man. You are but a foreigner here. You can shout African unity to the marines, it's but a mockery in practice. Keep a level head, lest the Kato people seize the opportunity to give you hell. Most people in Kato are proud, but lazy. You have to push them to get the best out of them. Try to create an oasis of efficiency around you. I want you to know that the University is a bedrock of tribal politics and conflicts. Steer clear or you may be swept away in the whirl-wind. Remember, you are here to work. Mind what you say, lest you are misunderstood. Forget all about my preaching. Eat and be merry. I wish our brothers and sisters joining us a happy and successful stay in Kato.'

The applause which greeted Babajo's sermon was deafening. Dr Jungu took a swig from the ginger ale bottle by his side. The bar appeared inexhaustible, as drinks of all descriptions were freely circulated and consumed. Someone always took one drink too many. It was Mr Olupanko this time. He was a pious gentleman whom many had hoped might one day answer a call to the holy orders. His dream seemed to have come true earlier than expected. He drenched himself with beer, probably an attempt at self-baptism. He broke loose and pontificated:

'Go home, ye sinners. Obey the injunction of the good Lord. Eat, drink, and be merry. Help yourselves to more drinks. . .'

At first many people got carried away by these antics and cheered at Olupanko's misdemeanour. His embarrassed wife, however, quickly hushed him up and before a worse picture was painted, he was forcibly ejected from the gathering. Everyone realized that Nigerians were not short of white sheep, in their midst. As the shrill sound of the guitarist of the most popular high-life disc filled the air, Elder Babajo grabbed one of the women and did a slow, measured and graceful dance to bring the merry-making to an end. He cut his steps around the periphery of the gathering like a champion miler doing a lap of honour. He was greeted with an unprecedented ovation as he nodded in appreciation. What a wonderful evening!

'Welcome, master, your friend was here,' called Dende, the houseboy, as he greeted the Jungus on their return home.

59

'Who? Did he not leave his name?' asked Dr Jungu. Apparently, Dende's level of English was nothing to count on.

'He carried his name with him,' was the reply.

'Ah! don't be funny. Don't you understand simple English? Did he not tell you his name?'

'Oh! Oh! His name is one long African name, it nearly reached a mile.'

'I see. It's our friend Abarakasinya,' Dr Jungu said, turning to his wife.

'His name is indeed a mouthful,' he spoke again.

'Now, Dende, next time we have a visitor, let him write his name on that notebook hanging in the doorway. OK?'

'But, master, suppose it is a woman?'

'Man or woman use that same notebook.'

Dende was by no means a young man. He must be nearer fifty than forty. Yet, his 'masters' who were always an average of ten to fifteen years younger than himself stuck the level 'houseboy' on him. Poor Dende had no choice. Dende had no fixed hours of work. He worked almost sixteen hours a day, seven days a week, except for a four-hour off duty on Sundays to commune with the good Lord. Dende accepted his lot and the Pastor of his village parish confirmed this view every Sunday, saying:

'The weak, the poor, and the meek shall inherit the kingdom of God. The beggar goes to heaven. The rich man goes to hell. Death is not the end of everything. There is hope beyond death . . . .'

Dende was naive. Did he think the rich who feathered their own nests by their large offerings and *who* kept the parish going would be forgotten on the day of reckoning? Dende's pastor knew who paid the piper. His last prayer every Sunday was, 'may the Lord bless those who have come forward with their offerings this Sunday.'

He was always silent on the poor and the needy, who had nothing to give.

Dr Jungu felt that houseboys deserved a better deal. He could not understand the preaching by labour union leaders about dignity of labour and equitable distribution of the national wealth when they appeared so far removed from the sufferings of the workers that they claimed to serve. The 'house-boys' might do well to salvage themselves. What they needed was a labour union with good leadership, then the 'masters' would be awake to the fact that house-boys also deserve a decent measure of life. It would appear that Dr Jungu felt more sorry for Dende than he did for himself. The 'masters' were to blame. Most had no conscience. Their wives were probably worse, worse than slave drivers.

'Good night, sir,' greeted Dende at the end of a good day's effort. It was ten at night.

'Good night, Dende. Be sure you are here very early, otherwise you might catch hell with Madam.'

Dr Jungu got to class early the following morning. He impressed his students as a good lecturer. He was as methodical as the old bush schoolteacher. He set himself a task at each lecture, hence he hated unwarranted interruptions by students who wanted further explanations on any issue. He devoted the last ten minutes to answering questions and giving further explanations for the benefit of the slower students. Most topics were illustrated with audio-visual aids. This was most desirable since there was no university farm to carry out meaningful practical work. His approach was most effective.

Word soon got around amongst the students about Onaola's effectiveness as a lecturer. It was not long before they detected that he was also a fair examiner. He made sure that all scripts were returned to their owners after grading them. This was followed by a most helpful discussion designed to improve the worst performers. The student with the best answer to each question was made to read his script to the class. He thought this was the best way to assure everyone that the lecturer was fair. In one of these discussion classes, a student raised his hand as if he were going to ask a question and commented as follows:

'I am not one of the best in this class. I am not ashamed of this but I am satisfied with my performance and at my steady improvement since you started to lecture us. Before your arrival, many male students suffered at the hands of weak male lecturers who graded them down at the expense of the beautiful-looking female students for obvious reasons. Many a time, our suspicions were difficult to justify because the clever lecturers did not even make a mark on any of the answer papers. It appeared that you were given an A if he liked your face or a C or even a D if you were running after the same female student as he was. No girl ever got below a B, an obvious attempt to win them over. We even had so-called experts who read from textbooks word for word to us and got paid the salary of their African counterparts. I have decided to go the whole hog to assure you that the students appreciate all the good things you are doing here. We hope you will remain in this university for a long time to come. But. . . but. . .'

'But what?' shouted the whole class as if they were urging him to cough out the part of the sentence he was about to swallow.

'But our intelligence sources have strongly pointed at sabotage from the so-called experts against your noble ideals and not the least, your very existence at Serti. Be very careful, sir.'

The students cheered their friend lustily as they associated themselves with the sentiments expressed. Dr Jungu thanked them and promised to be above board at all times.

Jungu's popularity rose rapidly. He had just topped the list in the ballot to appoint seven members of the senate from his faculty. The 'experts' led by Dean Nada had done all in their power to prevent his election. They failed woefully. Although the faculty had a total of forty-five members, twenty of whom constituted the experts group Dr Jungu had gathered together an insurmountable thirty-two votes. Obviously, to prevent his election another time, it would be necessary to divide the Africans into factions. The experts would have to devise a strategy to foil his success.

Meanwhile Jungu realized that three Kato citizens on the academic staff of the faculty, namely Dr Carpenter and Messrs Tando and Wusam, were die-hard supporters of the 'experts'. They cringed for them to gain access to the important sources of patronage. They were appointed to every committee by Professor Nada and their fortunes waxed and then waned depending on who sat on the woolsack of deanship. Theirs was an island of privilege in a sea of hostility for the other Africans. The trio was indeed a potent force to reckon with in faculty politics. The 'experts' therefore decided that to succeed at Serti, their policy of rewarding the faithful, seducing the doubtful, and entrapping the powerful opponents of their authority must be ruthlessly pursued. They had identified Dr Jungu as the number-one enemy of progress, a man likely to remove the cobweb from the eyes of his fellow Africans. He had to be crushed.

A circular was issued from the dean's office inviting all members of the faculty to a seminar on the research projects of four members of the faculty. Dean Nada was first to review his project. He was followed by the other three lecturers in order of seniority: a rigid system of precedence was always maintained on such occasions. Comments on the projects were to be given after each lecturer had spoken. Many hands were up, but Dean Nada asked Dr Jungu, who sat directly opposite him in the front row, to speak for fear that he might be accused of partiality. He began:

'I have basic comments to make. It will cut across all projects. I observed that a piecemeal approach is being adopted in treating the faculty research programme. The research programmes are neither published nor a report even demanded from the executors in knowing what had gone before so as to avoid unnecessary duplication of effort and a waste of the meagre financial resources at our disposal. Kato is not a rich country. We as scientists are expected to be reasonable and frugal. We need to relate our research to the current social and economic needs of the average man in Kato, emphasis being placed on applied and adaptive rather than on funda- mental research. What we need most urgently is a research committee to co-ordinate all research activities in the faculty with a view to solving clearly defined problems. If all the four of you who have presented your programmes were to get the go ahead to pursue your projects, it means that $75,000 out of a total allocation of $90,000 for this year will be appropriated by just four out of forty-five staff members. This will no doubt cripple the work of other lecturers. May we therefore resolve to shelve this review and address ourselves to getting a research committee first.'

Professor Nada fumed and regretted that he had not ruled Dr Jungu out of order earlier. The dean felt that as chairman he was privileged to silence an errant member of the flock by banging his gavel. Every step the Dean took that night was misplaced. Before dispersing, the faculty had voted by a staggering thirty to two with thirteen abstentions to approve the setting up of a faculty research committee. It was to consist of thirteen members: one each from the seven departments of the faculty, a representative each of the other four deans in the university; a representative of the president of the university, but with the dean of the faculty as chairman. All the thirteen who abstained comprised the 'experts'. Without approval from the faculty however, Dean Nada went ahead to initiate his programme. He alone had appropriated $60,000 for his research, two-thirds of the entire allocation for the year.

The date for the election to the faculty research committee was announced. The usual election fever gripped the faculty members. The 'experts' had decided to undermine Dr Jungu. Their strategy was simple: to nominate a reliable African candidate from the department of horticulture and back him to the hilt with the twenty 'experts' votes.

They figured that their stooge, if nominated, must be able to win convincingly against Dr Jungu. Dean Nada summoned Dr Carpenter and Messrs. Tando and Wusam to his office and lectured them like kids on the importance of keeping that devilish Jungu out of everything. He reminded them that it was not in their interest to allow a foreign African to lord it over them. He promised that his twenty experts would vote solidly for whoever was agreed upon as a suitable candidate. Dr Carpenter advised that Mr Wusam, a coastal man, stood the best chance, as ten other lecturers were from his area.

The day of elections had arrived, but the 'experts' did not reckon with the organizing ability of Dr Jungu. The meeting was called to order and Dean Nada stated in only five sentences why everyone was gathered there. He announced what was regarded a departure from the usual practice of nominating candidates for each department by members of that department; instead the whole faculty would vote for the candidates. He proposed that whoever obtained the highest vote should represent his department on the committee. Jungu had anticipated that Dean Nada would again resort to this kind of decisional autonomy. He had countered this effectively. He had got the seven other Kato men, one Briton, an Asian, and himself, to agree to nominate five candidates; the two stooges Carpenter and Wusam; the only 'expert' in the department, Professor Blake; one Briton and, of course, their beloved Jungu. While Jungu's supporters had tidied up their strategy and were all fully informed about it, Dean Nada revealed his plan only to the inner circle of experts - the heads of departments. Jungu's supporters also agreed not to cast a single vote for any other candidates nominated other than Jungu himself. The idea was to get the 'experts' and their supporters to split their votes. It was estimated that Jungu needed only fourteen votes to win.

'May I have your nominations please for the representative of the department of horticulture,' announced Nada.

'I beg to nominate Dr Jungu.'

'Any seconder?' asked Dean Nada.

Five others raised their hands in support. Promptly, four other nominations were made, as previously planned. Dean Nada, apparently feeling upset by the large number of nominated candidates, asked that Mr Tando collect and count the ballot papers when voting was completed. Dean Nada trembled on seeing the scorecard which read: Dr Jungu - 18; Mr Peabody - 10; Professor Blake - 7; Mr. Wusam - 6; and Dr Carpenter - 4.

It was obvious that none of the experts had voted for Dr Jungu, but he definitely enjoyed the support of about eight percent of all other members of the faculty and certainly that of all but three of those in his department. Things cooled off gradually. Before long the latest triumph of Dr Jungu had become history.

From then on, Dr Jungu directed his efforts at making concrete contributions to the university. Dean Nada had asked him to submit a research programme for funding by the university. This he did after an extensive tour of Kato and the fruit industries to ascertain their production problems. He submitted a modest three-year programme requiring $20,000 to implement. He hoped to meet part of the costs in kind through free supply of necessary fungicides from friendly European manufacturers.

Dr Jungu waited for three months, yet Professor Nada refused to submit the programme for review and approval by the faculty research committee. He therefore decided to forge ahead. He established a makeshift nursery by underbrushing a forest and used the shade provided by the tall trees. With his own money, he built a mud kolanut propagator. It looked rough and crude but proved effective. He had been told by a student, of a Kolanut tree (*Cola nitida*) which yielded over a thousand nuts annually. It was some 15 kilometres away from Serti. Dr Jungu observed the kola tree for about three months and certified it healthy since it appeared free of endemic diseases prevalent in the area. He went there early on a Sunday morning, took cuttings from just maturing flushes. He placed them in a bucket of cold water and covered them with a sack. By seven-thirty he had returned to Serti and set one hundred and twenty cuttings in the propagator. He watered them gently but thoroughly that day, and twice daily thereafter.

The students had co-operated fully on the project. They had realized that Dr Jungu was neither provided with a labourer nor an assistant. He was not even allocated a cent to expedite any project. It was all self-effort. A watering roster was prepared and the students kept religiously to it. Between the eighth and tenth week after setting the cuttings, eighty-five percent had rooted. These were carefully lifted, potted in locally woven palm-frond baskets, and watered adequately until the following rainy season when they were transplanted into the field. Again the students had assisted Dr Jungu in field preparation and planting. Such was their dedication that Dr. Jungu wished he could remain in Serti indefinitely. Ninety luxuriant, dwarf-sized kola trees still stand in Serti, a testimony to Dr Jungu's invaluable contribution to the department of horticulture's teaching aid. The trees also represent valuable, uniform clonal materials for research purposes.

Before long, Dr Jungu's contributions to his department were evident. He authored two books of forestry research in Africa, published an up-to-date review on the status of horticulture in Kato, initiated the students agricultural society in the university and formed the Planters' Society, the first of its kind in the history of Kato. He was also honoured with an appointment as a consultant to the All-African Forestry Programme of the Organization of African Unity. Dr Jungu's success must have confounded Dean Nada and his 'expert' friends. By way of contrast, the experts utilized ninety percent of the research fund but had no results of note to show for this colossal investment. This was probably why government functionaries in Kato became sceptical about further investment in forestry research.

6

CAMPUS GOSSIPS

Serti is a tiny village with no recreational facilities to boast of. The university authorities were fully conscious of this and their obligation to the staff. A modest senior staff club with a hard court for lawn tennis, an open field for children to run around, and a clubhouse with facilities for table tennis, billiards, a bar and restaurant was built. Exhibiting the usual colonial mentality, it was forbidden for any junior staff to enjoy these facilities. A large hall had been erected close to the junior staff quarters. There, the junior members of staff were shown films on the last Friday of every month at a nominal charge of five cents per family. That being the only form of evening entertainment, the junior staff looked forward to the occasion, not minding the fact that some of the films were made over twenty years earlier. For people who had not seen better things, it was better than nothing.

The senior staff club was the place to pick up the latest gossip on campus. It was heavily patronized by the 'experts.' One of the most regular customers was Dr Harry, Associate Professor and head of the department of forest botany. He was forty-six years old, with three children, but separated from his wife. He was a man with good basic educational qualifications but hardly any university teaching experience.

He had been, however, a distinguished artilleryman in the United States Army during the Korean Campaign. He ran around with many African girls and made the senior staff club his second home.

Dr Harry's first visit to the senior staff club made big news at Serti. He went straight to the bar and ordered a cold beer. As Richard, of Nigerian origin and better known as Dick among the regular club visitors, brought a glass of clear, golden ice-cold beer, Dr Harry exclaimed:

'Don't you ever serve frothing beer here?'

'Sorry, sir, I will change it for you.'

Dick disappeared into the small store behind the bar and quickly poured the same beer into another clean glass. It frothed so much that most of it was overflowing by the time he returned to Dr Harry.

'By Jove, that's real good beer. How much do I pay for it?'

'Only ten cents, sir.'

'Have twenty-five cents, twenty for the beer and five for you as reward for a good job done.'

'Thank you, sir.'

Dick giggled and invited the attention of Dr Jungu. He moved close to him and whispered into his ear:

'Brother, these experts must have more money than sense.'

'Why do you think so?'

'That doctor has only just paid double the price for the same stale beer which I poured very quickly into another glass.'

'Are you surprised at his attitude? Wouldn't you throw some money around too if you were privileged to be in his shoes?'

'Maybe. One of them was even reputed to have turned on the four air conditioners in his house throughout a three-month vacation when he and his family were away in America.'

'And who paid the bill?' asked Dr Jungu.

'It must be part of the help they are giving to Kato.'

'Dick, you are probably unaware of the reasons behind the action of the minister of finance in increasing the tax paid by you and me.'

'Do you mean we are paying for all that?'

'Precisely.'

'Master, you have opened my eyes today. So these people don't pay tax nor pay for light and water consumed. Who is actually giving the other assistance, we or they?'

'That's a million-dollar question?'

Dick noticed someone who appeared to be unfamiliar with the layout of the clubhouse roaming around. Dick took permission from Dr Jungu and left the bar.

'Can I help you?'

'Nothing is wrong with me. I am only looking for my master Dr Jungu,' stated Dende.

'Follow me. He is at the bar.'

'Has he now turned a drunkard?'

'He has tasted nothing yet. He is merely keeping our company.'

'You mean he is now working for your company.'

'No. He is having a chat with us.'

'Oh, oh. He is drawing maps at the club. His house should be more comfortable for that though.'

Realizing that Dende's spoken English was not good enough, Dick waved him to follow across the main hall of the club. As they got a clear view of the bar, Dr Jungu recognized Dende and inquired:

'Anyone looking for me?'

'Yes, sir. It's one old man. He came there before.'

'That must be Babajo.'

'No sir. This man is really old, but I don't know his name.'

71

'Is he short?'

'But everyone is tall, sir. No one is ever so many metres short,' corrected Dende.

'Dende, there you are again taking everything for a joke. How tall is he?'

'About as high as the rose plant in front of the house.'

'That's about two metres. It must be Pa Amodu.'

'You are right, sir. That's what he called his name.'

'Dende, run home. I will be there in another ten minutes. Meanwhile cook some rice and palava sauce. That's Pa Amodu's favourite dish.'

Dende hurried back to the house and served Pa Amodu some peeled oranges. They were delicious. Pa Amodu even chewed the spongy layer surrounding the juice sacs after sucking the juice therein.

'Pa Amodu, it's nice to see you again,' greeted Dr Jungu on returning home.

'I have some hot news for you. A visitation to be headed by Professor Garrinder is soon to review the administration, research and the organizational structure of our faculty. This may be an opportunity to change a lot of the unpleasant and unusual things going on in the faculty.'

'That's kind of you Pa Amodu. I hope the team will not consist of only Americans.'

'They will be British. They too want to give our faculty aid.'

'Beware, aid these days is full of strings.'

Pa Amodu, confident that he could explain it off and allay Dr Jungu's fears argued:

'It is in our own interest to take as much from these people as we can. They have siphoned so much wealth from our continent that a million-dollar grant per day cannot redeem the situation. They always say Africans are poor, but we all

72

know Africa is rich or else they won't be here. You ever see any poor white man in Africa?'

'Pa Amodu, enough of that philosophy. Let's go to table.'

'The food looks good,' said Pa Amodu as he drew out his chair by the dining table.

'Well, I cannot guarantee that it will taste well, as looks can be deceptive. Dende is only an average cook. Madam and the children are away for the weekend.'

The food was a little too salty and Pa Amodu did not hide the fact that he did not enjoy it. Pa Amodu told many stories including those about the fight for independence of Kato. Dr Jungu discovered from his long speech that Pa Amodu was a descendant of one of the greatest warriors of Kato. His great grandfather ruled a third of Kato at the turn of the twentieth century. Pa Amodu decided to while away the time rather than eat his food. He would not mind being excused because the situation was becoming embarrassing.

'Pa Amodu, how come you are not eating well today?'

'Brother, when Madam cooked, the food spoke for itself, but I assure you I had to speak for Dende's food.'

Dr Jungu could not help laughing. Old Pa Amodu was certainly witty and full of humour.

During the last term of the session, the long expected visitation headed by Professor Garrinder arrived at Serti University. Professor Garrinder was a distinguished forester with over twelve years' meritorious service in Nigeria. There he had established a close and cordial working relationship with Dr Jungu. He was expected at least to feel he had one friend at Serti. Jungu, to his dismay, discovered that blood was thicker than water. Professor Garrinder had decided to cast his lot with his white 'expert' brothers. He was adequately briefed on arriving in Serti by Dean Nada, who seized the

73

advantage to assassinate Dr Jungu's character. Obviously, Jungu must have been called names.

The red carpet was, as usual, laid for this visiting dignitary. Professor Garrinder was to meet members of each department individually. Dean Nada and Professor Blake accompanied him to the office of every member of the horticulture department, except to Dr Jungu's.

'What a pleasant surprise, you mean, you are here.'

'Nice to see you again,' replied Dr Jungu.

'I am a bit upset since I understand you have been up to a lot of mischief, complaining about everything in the faculty rather than being productive,' stated Professor Garrinder tactlessly.

'I am surprised that you have swallowed their evil propaganda hook, line, and sinker. I am also disturbed by your stand so soon after arriving in Serti. If only you will keep an open mind maybe I can re-establish my reputation with you,' explained Dr Jungu.

Jungu pulled out the top shelf of his rusty filing cabinet and brought out a file containing his activities since arriving in Serti barely seven months earlier. He displayed his publications and later drove Professor Garrinder to the kola farm he was establishing. The nursery was well kept and Professor Garrinder shook his head in disbelief and commented:

'Your achievements for an African operating under these stinkingly unbearably circumstances are exceptional. I am glad you are still the courageous gentleman who made do with meagre resources. Your output certainly has not been limited by lack of financial provisions.'

'But then, why did Dean Nada and Professor Blake not come with you to hear the sincere comments of an eminent scientist on my work? I hope you will henceforth address yourself to your assignment and help to silence forever our Doctors Know-all who have nothing to show for their fat pay. I personally believe that they are here to render assistance to Kato not with a view to removing their assistance, but to perpetuate dependence on them,' reaffirmed Dr Jungu.

Professor Garrinder left his office satisfied with what he had seen.

'You will figure prominently in my report,' he concluded.

Dr Jungu returned to the club that evening at the invitation of a few friends. It was members' night and there would be some dancing and 'suya.' There was Dr Harry who had engaged a girl in rhythmic dancing to the tune of the latest high-life music. As usual, he had come for the fun. Dr Jungu and his friends settled down to some Coca Cola at one end of the main hall of the club.

They talked and laughed over the exchanges between Professors Jungu and Garrinder. The news had spread like wildfire. Dr. Harry and his girl friend strolled past their table when the music stopped.

'Hi, Dr. Harry,' called Dr. Jungu.

'Hey, what are you doing in that corner? Would you have a beer on me?'

'No thanks. I am still struggling with some Coca-Cola. I have resolved never to taste alcoholic drink anymore.'

'What a resolution! You don't appreciate what you will be missing.'

Dick the barman interrupted this exchange and whispered into Dr Jungu's ears that Pa Amodu was waiting for him under a tree near the south end of the clubhouse. He took leave of his friends and located Pa Amodu with little difficulty.

'How are you and your family?'

'Fine,' replied Pa Amodu in a low voice.

Please talk louder; the music from the hall seems to be drowning your voice.'

'Not me. The walls have ears. Listen carefully, the dean is trying to get the president to appoint another 'expert' who obtained a masters degree just three years ago as a senior lecturer and member of the Senate.'

'Impossible, not as long as I am around.'

'He will get it through,' Pa Amodu assured.

'When will the matter be brought up for consideration by the Appointments and Promotions Committee?'

'Next Tuesday when you should be away to Buktu for an appointment with your doctor.'

'These guys must be good schemers.'

'Why not telephone your doctor postponing your visit?'

'But the telephone operator is one of their agents. Don't you know that she is Dr Harry's girlfriend?'

'You are damn right. You mean one of them.' Pa Amodu grinned. He continued, 'why not spring a surprise?'

'Pa Amodu, not this time. Not at the expense of my health.'

'I regret that you will fall an easy prey to these 'experts.''

'You want me to die and not be around to fight another time?' queried Dr Jungu. 'Don't forget that he who gambles with his health must bet his life. Me, I haven't a case of lives. I must travel to Buktu on Tuesday.'

'Well, a wise man solves his own problems. By the way, the meeting on Tuesday is scheduled for three o'clock in the President's office.'

'Immense thanks. Pa Amodu, what would I do in Kato without your good self?'

As Dr Jungu rejoined his friends, Dr Harry made for their table and said jokingly:

'I notice you have been out for almost thirty minutes. Were

76

you consulting with your African juju because I expect you to come up with something spectacular in a few days.'

'Are you afraid, or why that question?'

'Honestly, your disappearance raised some suspicion.'

'Nothing serious. I have diarrhoea so I went to the toilet.'

'You mean that kept you out for so long?'

'Certainly. I have even decided to go to Buktu for a medical check-up on Tuesday.'

'Haven't you heard the rumour that the Appointments and Promotions Committee will be meeting that afternoon?'

'Is that so, but remember my health counts first above anything else.'

'Poor you, we shall miss you.'

'Come on, you mean it's happy riddance as you guys will push through many things which would not ordinarily have passed, with me around.'

'Cheer up, I wish you a speedy recovery,' concluded Dr Harry.

Dr Jungu remained at the club with his friends for another three hours. Dr Harry left just about the same time. He drove straight to Dean Nada's house to brief him about Dr Jungu's proposed visit to Buktu on Tuesday. Dean Nada, who was earlier upset about his sleep being disturbed, thanked Dr Harry for the valuable information. The next morning was Sunday. Most of the lecturers at Serti were Christians with a difference. Only a few attended the regular interdenominational services. It was fishing day for the 'experts'. Dean Nada was at the riverside by ten o'clock. A messenger arrived shortly afterward with a message from President Oranlola.

'A note for you, sir.'

Dean Nada tore it open hastily. President Oranlola had appointed him acting president as he, Oranlola, would be away to Buktu from Sunday afternoon to return by midday Tuesday. He was however advised to issue a circular on the president's behalf on Monday inviting members of the Appointments and Promotions Committee to a meeting at three o'clock on Tuesday afternoon.

'All right. Thank the president for me.'

'Goodbye, sir.'

Turning to his wife Agnes, Dean Nada remarked:

'Mr Little will certainly be confirmed as senior lecturer for which I intend to recommend him.'

'Did you have any doubts about that?' queried Agnes.

'With Professor Jungu around it will not pass. You see he scrutinizes and reads very carefully every supporting document for a meeting. That's why he often comes up with objections that cannot be easily over-ruled.'

'How then do you hope to prevent him from attending the meeting?'

'You remember I got up from bed around midnight yesterday. Dr Harry came to drop a hint that Professor Jungu would be away to Buktu to see his doctor on Tuesday.'

'What a coincidence! Don't issue the circular until around ten o'clock on Tuesday.'

'That's a good suggestion. It won't even come out before noon to ensure that no one gets a telephone call across to him.'

'You mean he may rush back?'

'Agnes, it takes four hours from Buktu to Serti. Don't leave anything to chance.'

'I see the wisdom in your approach.'

To Dean Nada the new approach was foolproof. Dr Jungu, suspecting Nada's obvious plan, decided to really fool him. Late on Monday afternoon, he submitted a letter to his head of department for permission to be away on Tuesday for a

78

medical check-up at Buktu. Professor Blake was not keen on recommending it to the dean for approval since Dr Jungu might have to skip a lecture scheduled for five to six o'clock that evening. Pleading that he had arranged with the students to postpone it to between eight and nine o'clock on Tuesday night, Professor Blake picked up his telephone receiver and consulted the dean on the request.

'Hi, Professor Jungu would like you to approve a visit to his doctor on Tuesday. Honestly I don't recommend approval as he has to lecture that evening.'

'Please approve it. I will explain my reasons later. Do you mind if I talk to him?'

Professor Blake faked a smile and passed the telephone receiver to Dr Jungu:

'Hello, Dean Nada.'

'I am awfully sorry to hear that you are not feeling well. Please cheer up. You have my permission to be away on Tuesday. You may even stay on till Wednesday if necessary.'

'Thanks for your generosity. I should be back with the mail van around seven o'clock Tuesday evening. May I bring the request into your office for your signature?'

'You will be most welcome.'

As Dr Jungu reached the office of the secretary to the dean, Pa Amodu approached him and stated that the dean had left instructions that he was not going to see anyone else that day.

'Please telephone him. He asked me to come,' pleaded Dr Jungu.

Pa Amodu, at first reluctant for fear that he might be scolded by the dean, did as requested. Dean Nada came out and appeared most sympathetic. He promptly initialled his approval on Dr Jungu's note of request. He thanked the dean and drove straight home.

A few minutes before five o'clock, when the office was about to close, Pa Amodu took the stencils for the Appointments and Promotions Committee meeting to the dean for his signature. He had thought he could run them for distribution thereafter.

'Amodu, I will sign it, but don't cyclostyle them till noon on Tuesday,' instructed Dean Nada.

'But won't it be too late, sir?'

'Late? It is deliberate so we can keep Professor Jungu out of the meeting. Haven't you heard that he will be off to Buktu the whole of Tuesday to see his doctor?'

'I see. It's a good idea, sir.'

'Wise old Amodu, we have identical minds always.'

'Trust me, sir. I shall implement your instructions to the letter.'

Tuesday morning came and no one saw Dr Jungu on the campus. He had locked his garage to hide his car from view. The experts were sure that he had indeed travelled to Buktu. He and his wife cracked expensive jokes on how the 'experts' were likely to react when he would show up at the meeting.

'Dean Nada will blush and almost collapse,' observed Aida.

'I will turn a medicine man to revive him,' replied Dr Jungu.

'Take some APC with you as he is likely to complain of headache thereafter.'

'I'll pick up a bottle of APC from the dispensary, my dear.'

'That's a good idea since you may have three patients on your hands - Nada, Blake and Harry.'

'Aida, you are in excellent mood today,' he laughed.

The next morning, it was still drizzling when it was time for Olu and Bunmi to go to school. As they ran to the garage in an attempt to get into their father's car, Aida called them and advised that they would have to walk to school since their father·had travelled to Buktu. This was the routine anytime Dr Jungu travelled to Buktu in the university mail van as Aida was not licensed to drive a car. The children accepted the realities of the situation, ran back into their room to put on their raincoats, and set out for the school a little earlier than usual so as to get there in good time. Olu and Bunmi were just halfway to school when Dr Alamo's car suddenly pulled up by their side. The children were scared stiff.

'Hello, children,' greeted Dr Alamo. 'Do you care for a ride?'

'Thanks,' Olu replied on behalf of his brother and himself.

Dr Alamo carefully opened the door and asked the children in. As he drove on, he asked:

'Why do you have to walk to school on such a rainy day?'

'Our dad left for Buktu early this morning,' they replied.

'Buktu? To do what? Has he forgotten the important Appointments and Promotions Committee meeting at three o'clock?'

At first both children stared at each other totally ignorant of the issues raised by Dr Alamo. All of a sudden, Olu volunteered a reply:

'Daddy was not feeling well yesterday. I overheard him telling Mummy that he would have to see his doctor today at Buktu.'

'What a day to be sick! Well, children, I hope you have enjoyed the ride. I have to hurry to my lecture. Have a good day.'

Although the children did not understand the implications of Dr Alamo's comments, they reported what had happened to their mother on returning home.

'It's all right. He was only trying to pull your legs,' said Aida.

'Mummy, but our legs are short,' exclaimed Bunmi the older of the two boys.

'Boys, it's all a joke,' confirmed Aida.

Dr Jungu had had an early lunch so he did not go to the table with his family. He had hidden in his room for the entire time. At a quarter to three, he collected the key to his car, sneaked out of the house and drove to the president's office. He parked his car in a most unusual place, totally out of view. He disappeared into the finance office only to show up two minutes after the meeting had started.

'What happened?' shouted a completely baffled Dean Nada.

'I took some sleeping tablets and overslept,' replied Dr Jungu.

'By Jove, you should have come for a faculty Landrover. If it is not too late you can still have it. Remember health is wealth.'

'Thanks. I would rather travel on Wednesday. I feel very weak now. I don't think I am fit enough to stand the rough road in a Landrover.'

'But tomorrow Dr Harry will be using the Landrover.'

'If I drive to Buktu now, how will it be available for his use on Wednesday?'

'Let's drop the matter and continue with this meeting. Gentlemen, pardon me for the digression,' concluded Dean Nada.

After the Registrar had distributed the agenda and the curriculum vitae of the candidates, the Chairman granted members of the committee fifteen minutes to read through the papers.

'Gentlemen, may I call this meeting to order. For item one on the agenda, I propose that we consider Mr Little for the post of senior lecturer,' said Dean Nada.

'I'd like to second that proposal,' stated Professor Blake.

'Mr Chairman, may I suggest that we try to be objective. Mr Little obtained a master's degree just three years ago. If

82

he were African, he would have been made an assistant lecturer. In view of Mr Little's advanced age, however, let's honour him with the post of a lecturer,' suggested Dr Jungu.

'I associate myself with the views expressed by Dr Jungu. I have been here only three months and have observed frustration among African lecturers owing to the double standard adopted in appointments and promotions. It's time to call a halt to this disgraceful approach. Let's remember that this is a university community,' concluded Dr Debre.

All the other three deans supported the stand taken by Dr Jungu. Thoroughly displeased, Dean Nada called for more comments. 'Let's remember that anything short of senior lecturership will prevent Mr Little from becoming a member of the academic board.' Professor Blake explained further.

'Arrant nonsense! A gunner from the army taking up a job in the university for the first time as a senior lecturer. Not on my life. He has no publications either. By the way, what was he before coming here?' asked Dr Debre in annoyance.

'A forestry extension agent,' replied the chairman.

'Then let's call him forestry extension expert,' suggested Dr Jungu.

'Forestry extension expert/lecturer,' was Dr Debre's amendment.

'That's even better. I accept the amendment,' stated Dr Jungu.

'Since there are no opposing views, Mr Little is appointed forestry extension expert/lecturer,' concluded Dean Nada, the chairman.

Other appointments were less controversial. In another twenty minutes, the meeting was over. While Dean Nada and his lieutenants left the meeting disappointed, other members of the committee rejoiced that a sensible decision had been taken. They hoped this was the beginning of the normalization of events on campus. News of the latest triumph over the evil machinations of the experts spread quickly over the campus. Many African lecturers congregated at the senior staff club later that evening to toast the victory, but no one reckoned with the weakness of President Oranlola. He seemed to be under the thumb of the American experts. Seven months later, during the long vacation, President Oranlola was pressurized to review the decision.

A proposal to supply teak seedlings to all farmers in Kato participating in the extensive afforestation projects to be financed by the American Assistance Programme had been shown to President Oranlola by Dean Nada. A sum of one hundred thousand dollars was needed for the satisfactory execution of the project.

There had been a cautious welcome to the announcement by Dean Nada that the American Assistance Programme would make the grant of one hundred thousand dollars to Kato for the project and that the faculty of forestry and horticulture of Serti University had been appointed the executing agents for the project. Other clauses in the carefully worded agreement provided for a project manager of American origin, but who should not be below the rank of associate professor.

'Mr President, it would appear cheaper to appoint someone who is already a member of our faculty to the post of project manager rather than request the American Assistance Programme for a new professor from America for this purpose. Mind you, the salary and allowances of the new man will eat deep into the one hundred thousand dollars, thus making it virtually impossible to accomplish the task we have set ourselves,' suggested Dean Nada.

'But Mr Little, who would have been ideal as project

manager, is still very junior in status. Can't Dr Harry be assigned the duty?' suggested President Oranlola.

'A forest botanist to undertake the work of a forestry extension expert? Certainly not. The cap fits Mr Little. Moreover, he is American. Why don't you promote him?' advised the dean.

'From lecturer to associate professor all within one session? I hope you don't want to make me a laughing stock of the academic world,' noted the President, opposing the suggestion vehemently.

'But Serti University is not responsible for paying Mr Little's salary and allowances. The American Assistance Programme is already taking care of that. Mr Little needs the change in status to boost his ego,' remarked Dean Nada.

'How do I justify this unique advancement to the Board of Trustees of the University? Mind you, I am answerable to them.'

'Mr President, the bargain is clear, it's Mr Little or no one else. If you decide otherwise, the American Assistance Programme will certainly have to freeze the grant. Moreover, tell the board of trustees that it is a new appointment not a promotion, and that at the expiration of the time when applications were called for, it was only Mr Little who had applied for the post. Explain that it was a *fait accompli*,' Dean Nada rocked with laughter.

'One hundred thousand dollars is a lot of money. Mr Little will have to be-upgraded rather than for me to lose the money,' agreed the president most reluctantly.

The next day, an extraordinary circular was issued by the office of the President stating:

Under the powers conferred on me by section **8, clause** (iii) of the constitution of Serti University, I, Dr Samuel **Oranlola**, by the Grace of God the President of the University, **hereby** appoint Mr Little, formerly Forestry Extension Expert in the Faculty of Forestry and Horticulture, to the post of Associate Professor in the same Faculty and Project Manager of the Kato Afforestation Programme with immediate effect.

As if it had long been anticipated, the signboard at the entrance to Mr Little's residence was removed and replaced within an hour of the release of the circular with a more appropriate one reading 'Prof. Roland Little.' Professor Little celebrated his undeserved upliftment in a big way. All the experts and their wives gathered in his house that night. Till dawn they wined and danced to the music of the latest soul tunes. As expected, there was dissatisfaction in the African quarters and elsewhere with the latest triumph of the experts. A concerted effort would have to be made to check these ugly tendencies that appeared to damage the erstwhile good reputation of the university.

7

CLASH WITH NADA

Professor Nada had decided to destroy Dr Jungu's enviable image at all costs. He was afraid that Professor Garrinder"s report might uphold Dr Jungu's views and thus convert more adherents to his cause. For self-pre-servation, he had resolved to crush Dr Jungu by using all means at his disposal, save African *juju*. He had decided to employ the services of Dr Carpenter, and Messrs. Tando and Wusam as a front. They were to fight him, sabotage his efforts, and assassinate his character to frustrate him. Backbiting raged like wildfire. The trio, a group of slippery cowards, represented forces of evil and selfishness. Dr Jungu was aware of their plot. He was battle-ready and had resolved never to be battle-weary until sanity was restored to faculty life.

The usual bait had been thrown at Mr Tando, lecturer in wood technology. He readily swallowed it. He was appointed acting head of the department of wood technology starting from the beginning of the long vacation in June. This was a reward for the faithful Tando, but it was short-lived. Mr Tando was not given full operational authority. His actions had to be endorsed by Dean Nada and all letters issuing from him had to be countersigned by the dean as well. It had been felt in some quarters that this was a device to befall a 'good boy,'

87

but Mr Tando soon realized that this was because Dean Nada was not convinced he could do the job satisfactorily without close supervision. Moreover, this approach ensured that the department was run the way Dean Nada wanted.

At this time, the real estate industry of Kato was enjoying an unprecedented boom and the department of wood technology released various types of sawn planks and plywood into the market. People queued every Tuesday and Thursday to make purchases. By September, just before the new session had started, losses to the tune of $10,000 had been recorded by the department under Mr Tando's administration. Dean Nada held his now famous informal consultation with the president and, by next day, Mr Tando had been cut down to size. He was relieved of his appointment as acting head of the department.

As if by design, Mr Campbell had returned from leave the previous day. The next move was anybody's guess. He was reappointed acting head of the department. The plan was perfect. The department had envisaged fairly high financial losses during Mr Campbell's absence, otherwise there would have been no justifiable reason for wanting to dislodge the 'good boy,' Mr Tando.

'Don't you worry,' consoled Dean Nada, 'you are sure of getting three increments by first of October.'

Dean Nada felt convinced on the other hand that he had proved his point that a Kato citizen was incapable of running a department successfully.

By November of the same year the blue-eyed boy, Mr Campbell, had recorded a staggering loss of $40,000 in the same department. Dean Nada with the president's approval summoned a meeting of the University Finance Committee to deliberate on his memorandum on the appalling financial situation of the wood technology department. He had recommended, among other things, an increase in prices of between twenty-five and fifty percent. He had calculated that by the following March, the departmental account would have broken even. Most members of the committee rejected his suggestion, but noted regrettably that Mr Campbell's ouster had not been recommended. Dean Nada resisted this move and threatened to resign his position first as a Professor and also as dean of the faculty. Feeling that they had made their point, the committee ratified a flat twenty percent increase in prices on all items produced for sale in the wood technology department.

Dr Jungu attacked the recent decision at the next academic staff meeting and wondered why double standards should be adopted for the 'experts' and Africans. Dr Jungu lashed out:

'To satisfy us and restore mutual confidence, Mr Campbell deserves to be relieved of his post for mismanagement too. Who the hell do you 'experts' think you are kidding? If I were Mr Campbell, I would cover my face in shame and resign voluntarily and honourably as head of department. Gentlemen, do not ask me why, if you do not already know as I do that Mr Campbell will sit tight like an African Governing Party politician just defeated at the polls. Your guess is as good as mine.'

Mr Tando and his associates met under a mango tree near the rest house later that evening to deliberate on Dr Jungu's efforts to bring fair play into the faculty. They were not sure whether Dr Jungu was merely enunciating principles of fair play or whether he had seized the opportunity to rub it in on the 'experts.' They were at least convinced that he was courageous. Thinking that they were out of the dean's earshot, they predicted that at the rate things were shaping up on campus, in six months' time Dean Nada would either be forced to quit or Dr Jungu would have to leave Serti to save his skin.

The electricity plant of the university had suddenly broken down and within the next ten minutes, all the experts had congregated in front of Professor Blake's house, some thirty metres from the mango tree under which the Tando trio had stood. This was a ritual. They had gathered there every time the light went out like people who felt unsafe in a territory they ruled. What an irony of life. Dean Nada was the first to arrive, and before long he had discovered the Tando trio. He walked stealthily toward them as he did not want to be noticed. Mr. Wusam, whose roving eye surveyed the territory around them as a precaution, spotted him and quickly moved forward to pay his courtesies.

'What are you folks up to at this time of the night?' asked Dean Nada.

'Is the Ghost of Dr Jungu haunting you?'

'They all laughed heartily, but pretended that they had forgotten all about what Dr Jungu had said just as he finished speaking. They were agreed, however, that he was only blowing his top as usual.

'I trust that you are reasonable people. Never allow that unreasonable fellow to change your outlook. As long as I am here, you are assured a good future.'

With these words of encouragement, Dean Nada left them and rejoined his expert friends.

The few vocal members of the faculty grumbled loud for another three weeks or so about Mr Campbell's fate *vis-à-vis* that of Mr Tando. Everyone soon forgot all about it. Just then there was a new arrival from America - another 'expert.' He was a middle-aged gentleman with a B.Sc. in forestry and a Ph.D., also in forestry; the latter qualification was obtained only one year before joining the university. His status was to be determined and the seven-man Appointments and

Promotions Committee had been summoned for that purpose. Dean Nada rattled through the curriculum vitae of Dr Bandy in less than two minutes. Apart from his qualifications, his main asset was that he was a successful air force major during the Korean campaign. He had not seen the inside of a university lecture room save for when he himself was a student. Dean Nada concluded:

'I recommend this gentleman for the post of associate Professor in the department of forest pathology.'

'Impossible,' cried Dr Jungu. 'I hope Dean Nada wants this committee to take his recommendations seriously. Dr Bandy should be appointed a lecturer.'

Contributing to the discussion, Professor Blake naturally supported Dean Nada, claiming that anything short of associate professorship would prevent him from heading the department of forest pathology and representing the faculty at the senate.

Dr Debre, a French Professor at the university, bitterly attacked the views expressed by both Dean Nada and Professor Blake, stating:

'I want it recorded that I again oppose this proposal. It is this double standard that is ruining this institution. I hope you will all realize that most of the Africans on campus are suffering in silence. A change in attitude is long overdue. Last time it was Mr Little, now it is Dr Bandy. Mr President, sir, may I move that Dr Bandy be confirmed as a lecturer.'

All the other members of the committee except Professor Blake spoke in support of Drs Debre and Jungu.

The president decided to take the line of least resistance. He stated:

'I see that the majority view supports that Dr Bandy be made a lecturer. This is acceptable, but I intend to insert the words lecturer/adviser after his name in the university calendar. In addition, I intend to raise the issue at the next senate meeting as to whether Dr Bandy could not be co-opted under section 3 (v)(a) of the University Act.'

Since no one raised any further objections, the meeting was brought to a close.

The question of Dr Bandy's status had remained an unfinished business as far as the 'experts' were concerned. Dean Nada and his group needed him in senate to get a particular item passed. They waited for an opportune moment. Dr Jungu had travelled to neighbouring Shongaland as a consultant horticulturist for two months. Dean Nada promptly reopened the matter with the president and out came a circular signed by the president himself.

'Dr Bandy, an outstanding forestry expert from America, has been appointed a Professor of forest pathology with immediate effect. As the only person in that department above the status of senior lecturer, he automatically fills the vacancy for that department in the University Senate.'

Eight European lecturers in the faculty sent in letters of resignation to the president of the university the same afternoon the circular was issued in protest against the arbitrary decision of the president. They complained in their joint letter that they were not in a position to stand around while academic standards were being dashed to the dogs. To them, it was suspected that influences emanating from the 'expert' clique were trying to convert Serti University into a third rate college. This they thought should be resisted by all those who cherish high academic standards.

The president of the university, suspecting that some rash African lecturers might join in the resignation wave, ordered that all the eight lecturers quit the university within the next forty-eight hours. This action was later challenged by another group consisting of an Asian, a Dutchman, and two Africans. They forwarded a letter of protest to the board of trustees through the president following the normal communication channels. The petition had no effect as it was successfully suppressed by the president. In consequence, all the four petitioners also resigned. By March of the following year, a total of twenty-seven other lecturers, the bursar, chief pharmacist, chief engineer, and the domestic warden had resigned and left Serti.

The president held the view that this trend was not unusual in young African universities, although most people failed to share this view both within and outside the university.

Dr Jungu for once did not comment on the latest happenings. It was strange, but he was not surprised. He was, however, more concerned with the reorganization of his faculty administration. He believed that it would not be profitable to resign; it was better to remain and fight for what was right. He was encouraged by the fact that unlike most other African colleagues, he had permanent tenure as a full Professor of the university. With renewed vigour, he tabled a controversial topic for discussion at the next faculty board meeting. It was routed through Professor Blake, his head of department. He wanted the question of acting headship of departments and acting deanship of the faculty discussed.

Moments later, a messenger brought an invitation to join Dean Nada and himself for drinks at eight o'clock that night. This was an unusual invitation since the 'experts' kept strictly to themselves and never invited anyone else to their houses or to parties organized by any of them either alone or jointly. Curiosity demanded that Dr Jungu should honour the invitation.

'Peace be unto this house,' saluted Dr Jungu as he was

ushered into Professor Blake's house at a quarter to eight by the steward.

'Come on in,' replied Professor Blake, adjusting the knot of his tie.

'You have a colourful African dress on tonight. I bet that must be very expensive. In another five to ten minutes, Dean Nada should arrive. What would you like to drink?'

'I am not keen on having any drinks tonight. You know, I usually have dinner at seven o'clock. Maybe you carefully picked this time to save your drinks,' joked Dr Jungu.

'Here comes Dean Nada. He barely made it on time. It's two minutes past eight. May I have your jacket?' asked Professor Blake.

Dean Nada did not hide the fact that communications between him and Dr Jungu had been breaking down for upward of eight months. That was since Dr Jungu first criticized his research programme. Dr Jungu felt that Dean Nada must be narrow-minded. He was the type who resisted change at all costs. He believed the 'experts' were at Serti to rule. Dr Jungu had felt that Dean Nada of all people should have been very nice to him since one good turn deserves another. As soon as Dr Jungu accepted the offer of appointment with Serti University, Dean Nada entered into communication with him for kola 'raments.' These were rare commodities but Dr Jungu strained himself to get fifty for him three months before arriving at Serti. These plants now stand to the credit of Dean Nada at Serti, but not many were aware that without Dr Jungu's special efforts those valuable plants might never have got to Serti.

As if he was oblivious to the fact that this meeting had been prearranged by Dean Nada and himself, Professor Blake announced that he had decided to invite both of them with a

94

view to getting Dr Jungu to withdraw his proposal to discuss acting headships of departments and deanship of the faculty. He threatened that if Dr Jungu maintained his ground, he would prevent him from travelling to the conference of the African Fruit Grower's Association taking place in Accra, Ghana, to which he had been invited as a keynote speaker. Dr Jungu rocked with laughter since he had detected Professor Blake's ignorance on this issue. The president of the university had written Dr Jungu three days earlier conveying approval to him. Moreover, a return flight ticket had been issued and a generous per diem had been made available to him in dollar traveller's cheques. Dr Jungu said:

'Is this why you have brought me to your house, to threaten me and buy me over? I have justifiable cause to feel unsafe in these premises. Come what may, I shall not withdraw.'

Realizing that their mission was bound to fail, Professor Nada asked for a cold beer, maybe to cool down from the shock. Dr Jungu refused to taste anything. He bided his time and escaped from their grip before they made life more unbearable for him.

The next day, Dean Nada had issued a circular for the faculty board meeting scheduled for three of the same day, but without listing the topic suggested by Dr Jungu. Dr Jungu's reaction was sharp and prompt. He felt like a wounded lion. Within the next two hours, the original circular had been withdrawn and an amended one incorporating the item listed by Dr Jungu was published. Lecturers now expected a hot debate at the session.

The meeting was well attended. Each item was taken, considered, and decided by votes. When it came to item five, the item listed by Dr Jungu, Dean Nada used the chairman's privilege to transfer it to the end. By six o'clock, the dean suggested that in view of the fact that the last item was very controversial and realizing that three hours had already been devoted to the meeting, the faculty should consider adjourning for another week. Dr Jungu raised his hand to make a motion. He was granted the floor. He got support for continuation of the meeting by twenty-six votes to two, most of the 'experts' having refrained from exercising their voting rights. Thereafter, Dr Jungu was given the floor to introduce the topic.

'We have all witnessed the arbitrary way in which acting heads of departments and acting dean of the faculty have been appointed in the past. This is not the procedure adopted in the other faculties. Ours is unique. Lecturers have been appointed to serve in either capacity when senior lecturers, associate professors, and full professors were available. There was an attempt to cover up by the dean when he explained to me that he chose to be flexible over the matter to give Kato citizens a chance since most of them were only lecturers. I personally called his attention to the fact that of the five lecturers who had acted, only one was a Kato man. I need a change to avoid frustration.'

'Any comments?' asked Dean Nada.

Eight of the ten people who spoke supported Dr Jungu's demand. One 'expert' and Dr Carpenter, however, suggested that the *status quo* be maintained. Dean Nada, apparently taking the faculty members for granted, announced that the consensus was for the old system to continue. There was an uproar and one disgusted lecturer even reminded Dean Nada that they were tired, but not asleep! A young assistant lecturer then moved a motion to the effect that in view of the seriousness of the situation, a committee of five should be chosen to review the matter and submit recommendations within four weeks to another meeting of the faculty board.

96

The motion was seconded and was won comfortably by a wide margin when put to a vote. Dean Nada, appreciative of the fact that only the reformers might find their way into the committee if the normal democratic way was adopted, announced the names of his handpicked committee members: Mr Wusam (as chairman), Dr Carpenter, Dr Elijah, Dr Adams, and Mr Nosiru - all of them citizens of Kato. Dr Elijah was known as a moderate in the faculty. He held the balance since Wusam and Carpenter leaned very much to the dean's view, while Adams and Nosiru belonged to the group of latter-day reformers.

The Wusam committee met to map out a programme on how to tackle their assignment. It was unanimously agreed that a memorandum should be invited from each member of the faculty. Surprisingly, when the deadline for its submission had been reached, not one memorandum was put in. It was clear that no one was going to waste his time on what was considered obvious in view of the loud protests on the issue in the last four years since Professor Nada became dean. The committee next decided to interview each member of the faculty in his office. Again most lecturers did not cooperate for fear of being identified with the reformer group. Finally, the committee decided to interview the deans of the other four faculties and write to some African universities on the procedure for the appointment of deans of faculty and heads of department. The replies were collated and carefully studied. A preliminary report was produced after a solid four weeks of deliberation. Realizing that it was unable to meet the deadline for the submission of its report, the committee asked and was granted another four weeks extension to complete its assignment.

In an attempt to influence the recommendations of the committee, Dean Nada invited Mr Wusam to his office. He requested Mr Wusam to inform him of the highlights of the committee's recommendations. Mr Wusam revealed that it had been unanimously recommended that henceforth academic seniority be recognized and that acting appointments for headships of departments and acting deanship of the faculty should take due cognizance of that. He added that the committee also recognized the need for the creation of a post of vice-dean of the faculty to assist the dean in the execution of his duties. He said further that only people who were senior lecturers and above would qualify for election annually to the post of vice-dean of the faculty.

'Are you people sick in the head?' asked a bewildered Dean Nada.

'I hope that crank, you know him - Dr Jungu - has not been around pumping all sorts of stupid ideas into your heads. Your recommendations are a sell-out. You will have to change them all.'

'I am afraid it is rather late, sir, as the committee is unanimous on these principles,' retorted Mr Wusam, who for once summoned up courage to speak his mind in the presence of Dean Nada.

'That is outrageous,' fumed Dean Nada.

'Are you now becoming untrustworthy? It was not for fun that you got appointed as the chairman of the committee. You will have to persuade your committee to either water down the recommendations or plug in some safety valves to cut our number-one enemy to size at will at the earliest opportunity. You are toying with your destiny under the high ideals of democracy. Does it not occur to you that in any popular and fair election for vice-deanship, Dr Jungu will surely sweep the polls? I cannot stand him for one minute as my lieutenant.

Moreover, don't you appreciate the fact that as it now stands, Dr Jungu, the only other professor on the faculty apart from Professor Blake, becomes the automatic choice for acting deanship in view of his four weeks' seniority over Professor Blake? Go back to your committee and amend the recommendation for flexibility.'

'But what exactly would you want us to do, sir?' asked a worried Mr Wusam.

'My boy, it's simple. Since it appears your committee is bent on pushing through those recommendations, advise the committee to insert a clause that whenever someone acts for four weeks and over as a head of department, he should be subject to removal if three or more members of his department should express dissatisfaction with his leadership. I assure you, this is a necessary clause to ensure that Jungu would not have to run the horticulture department throughout the long vacation when Professor Blake is away in America on leave. For acting deanship, it is suggested that you insert a clause permitting the appointment of the only two professors in rotation. That will give me the privilege of appointing only Professor Blake when I am away for long periods,' concluded Dean Nada.

'We shall try our best,' assured Mr Wusam.

Mr Wusam was a bit upset not only by the dirty job he had been asked to do, but also by the fact that Dean Nada was so narrow-minded that he failed to address himself to principles rather than to individuals. To Dean Nada, the conflict between him and Jungu was to override the interests of the faculty. Much as Wusam could not see the wisdom in Dean Nada's reasoning, he felt bound to carry out Dean Nada's wishes since he held his post of chairman of the committee at Dean Nada's pleasure. Mr Wusam therefore summoned another

meeting of his committee for a critical look at their recommendations before submission to the dean. At the meeting,
which was attended by only four of the five members, Dr
Elijah being absent, Mr Wusam introduced the dean's suggestions as if they originated from him. He assured the committee that the two amendments would ensure flexibility and prevent a department or the faculty being headed by an unwanted
individual.

'I thought we were dealing with principles, not individuals.
Could you elaborate on this a little more?' asked an impatient
Dr Adams.

'If I must call a spade a spade, it should be obvious to you
all that our recommendations would favour Dr Jungu, who
will always act as dean in Dean Nada's absence and as head
of the horticulture department in Professor Blake's absence,'
explained Mr Wusam.

'What's wrong with that? Is he not a professor just like
Blake or Nada? What has Nada got to show for his four
years' stay here, anyway? A fat car, fat salary, and luxurious
living? A few of us seem to be afflicted with a warped
mentality. Let's not look ridiculous. I move that we stick to
our original recommendations,' proposed Dr Adams.

'I beg to oppose the motion,' stated Dr Carpenter. 'Instead
I wish to enter a countermotion to the effect that Mr Wusam's
wise suggestions be incorporated into the original
recommendations.'

'Any seconder for this motion?' asked Mr Wusam.
Since no one raised his hand in support, MrWusam himself
seconded the motion and asked for a vote on the countermotion
first. As expected, there was a tie of two votes each way. Mr
Wusam using his casting vote as the chairman swung the
pendulum in favour of Dr Carpenter's motion. And so Dean

Nada's views were inserted. The final recommendations adopted for presentation to the faculty therefore read:

PREAMBLE:

This Committee was appointed eight weeks ago to review the procedure for appointing acting headships of departments and acting deanship of the Faculty of Forestry and Horticulture and make recommendations to the Faculty Board.

The five members of the Committee were Mr Wusam (Chairman), Dr Carpenter, Dr Elijah, Dr Adams, and Mr Nosiru.

Seven meetings of the Committee were held and the following recommendations were unanimously approved for consideration by the Faculty Board.

RECOMMENDATIONS:

1. *General*

(a) The Committee unanimously recommends that academic seniority must be recognized in the faculty and due cognizance of this must be taken in all acting appointments within the faculty.

(b) When there is more than one person of equal academic seniority in a department or faculty, acting appointments shall be rotated amongst them with the Dean using his discretion as to who acts first.

(c) A Vice-Dean should be elected as soon as this report is accepted by the Faculty.

2. *Acting Headships of Departments:*
   (a) The most senior academic staff shall be appointed whenever there is a vacancy for acting appointments except that due considerations must be given for the provisions in clause 1 (b) above.
   (b) Whenever a staff member has acted for four weeks or more he shall be subject to removal by the Dean if three or more academic staff in his department were to petition the Dean on his inability to hold the department together.

3. *Acting Dean of The Faculty;*
   The most senior academic staff in the Faculty shall be appointed acting Dean except that the provisions in Clause 1(b) above shall be enforced when applicable.

4. *Vice Deanship:*
   (a) A Vice-Dean shall be democratically elected by the Faculty at the beginning of each session and he shall hold office for one year.
   (b) All senior lecturers, associate professors, and professor in the Faculty are eligible for election and shall be considered duly nominated in writing at least three days before the election.
   (c) A Vice-Dean shall be eligible for re-election after the expiration of his term of office.
   (d) The Vice-Dean shall assist the Dean in the day- to-day administration of the Faculty, but shall not be the automatic choice to act as Dean unless he is the most senior academic staff in the Faculty.

Members of the committee signed the report, and it was presented to Dean Nada by Mr Wusam, the chairman of the committee, on behalf of all the members. Dean Nada, pretending that he had never got wind of the contents of the Wusam report, thanked the committee for a job well done, stressing the fact that he was yet to read the report. Thereafter, Dean Nada kept the report for another three weeks, obviously waiting for an opportune moment to call a faculty meeting.

Meanwhile, Mr Wusam and Dr Carpenter at the instance of Dean Nada sought audience with the president of the University the same evening that the report was submitted to Dean Nada. They expressed fears to the president that if the recommendations in the report just submitted by Mr Wusam's committee were approved and implemented, they would end up having Dr Jungu as the alternate dean of their faculty.

'I think this a shame. You people were influential members of a committee and yet you signed and submitted a report containing views that you did not believe in. I am unable to assist you on this matter. Pray your faculty does not endorse your submission,' stated the president in disgust as he dismissed the two gentlemen.

On reporting that their effort to get the president to influence the recommendations in favour of Dean Nada had failed, Dean Nada framed up some new ideas to neutralize Dr Jungu.

'Gentlemen, I thank you for the efforts made so far, could you return to this house in another two hours?'

'John! John!!'

'Here, sir,' answered Dean Nada's houseboy, standing at attention in front of him.

'Take this note to Dr Alamo, the senior lecturer from Puerto Rico. I suppose you know his house.'

103

The front door bell rang and Dean Nada gracefully opened the door.

'Nice to see you, Dr Alamo.'

'It's indeed an honour to be invited to your lovely house,' he replied.

'What would you like for a drink?' Dean Nada asked as he ushered him into his living room.

'Gin and tonic, please.'

'To your health,' each person toasted as their glasses touched.

'By the way, have you seen the Wusam Report?'

'I only heard rumours that it has been submitted to you.'

'What? Just a minute,' Dean Nada exclaimed as he disappeared into his study. 'Glance through this copy if you please.'

'May I take it home so as to digest its contents?' requested Dr Alamo.

'Mark you, it is still a secret document. You must consider yourself privileged to see it now. At this stage, what is important is to read the recommendations.'

After some minutes of intensive concentration, Dean Nada asked Dr Alamo:

'If this report were adopted as it stands, who would you nominate for the position of vice-dean?'

'Dr Jungu,' was his prompt reply.

'You are still green here. Would you not consider Dr Jungu inflexible and unnecessarily strict?'

'Well, but he is the most senior of the possible contestants. Moreover he is also the most suitable.'

Sensing that efforts to persuade Dr Alamo to change his mind might prove abortive, he saw him out of his house before the return of Dr Carpenter and Mr Wusam.

During the brief meeting with Dr Carpenter and Mr Wusam,

a new plan was adopted by the trio in their efforts to dissuade as many faculty members as possible from nominating Dr Jungu for the post of vice-dean. Dean Nada cleverly decided to withdraw from the scene, thus leaving the over-zealous Mr Wusam and Dr Carpenter to do the trick.

Dr Adams was most displeased with what was going on and so he decided to bring everything to Dr Jungu's attention. Dr Alamo followed suit. Dr Jungu was so enraged that he almost decided to go to Dean Nada's office to give him a bit of his tongue. He controlled his temper, however. Instead of picking up quarrels, he decided to use pressure to get the Wusam report officially released.

Jungu, posing as a friend of the cheated and an advocate of the oppressed, went round the departments of the faculty informing all lecturers that there was an attempt to shelve the Wusam report as its findings had not favoured Dean Nada and his group of 'experts.' He reminded them that the report had been submitted five weeks earlier to Dean Nada and that if there was no concerted effort on the part of staff to get it discussed, it might end up in the waste paper basket just like any useless scrap of paper. Jungu's campaign soon won the support of most members of the faculty and many lecturers started to grumble aloud. People like Dr Blamo, a senior lecturer in the department of wood technology where the young, inexperienced Mr Campbell had been acting as head of department for the past fourteen months, joined forces with Dr Jungu. Dean Nada soon became apprehensive of a possible showdown. He could no longer hang on to the Wusam report. He set a date for a faculty meeting at which the report was to be discussed. The circular announcing this was most welcome.

'I beg to call this meeting to order,' stated Dean Nada as he banged the table with a gavel.

'You have all got a copy of the Wusam report. Your comments are now invited.'

There was dead silence in the board-room and one could have heard the sound of a pin had one been dropped. Faculty members stared at one another as if to ask who will bell the cat. This was the occasion that the so-called reformers had long waited for. Dr Jungu began to wonder in disbelief whether no one other than himself would speak. He prayed that this should not happen, as otherwise it might appear that he was the only discontented one on the faculty. But the authorities of Serti University had a clever device for keeping dissatisfied academic staff quiet. Such members of staff would rather suffer in silence than voice their opinions. As long as a member of the academic staff was below the rank of professor, his appointment was probationary for the first six years. This was an unbearably long period to remain a good boy, otherwise you offered yourself for slaughter like a culprit who has rubbed oil on his body and is found perching by the side of a huge fire. The president was often too eager to clamp down on any person considered a 'bad egg' in the university community. And it was easy to be labelled one. For instance, a constructive critic of the president's speech or actions is quickly asked to leave, with or without a month's salary in lieu of notice. President Oranlola was known to hide conveniently under the excuse that you were dismissed for state security reasons. This you cannot fight and win. Dean Nada, on the other hand, had a way of getting the president to deal a deathblow to any lecturer he considered undesirable and a threat to his authority. This by and large had been responsible for the unusually high turnover of staff on the faculty, thus perpetuating staff instability. Serious as the situation appeared to be, it did not occur to many that the people who suffered most in the drama were the helpless students.

Mr Nosiru, a young assistant lecturer who served on the Wusam committee, feeling that the faculty probably wanted some explanation on the report, offered a few comments. As expected, he solidly backed every clause of the report. To others, the ice had been broken. Others reasoned that if Mr Nosiru could come out so strongly for the report in a well-attended faculty board meeting, the authorities might have to slash down virtually all faculty members. Faculty members got up one after another praising the committee for a balanced report. Most speakers however, objected to clause 2(b) of the recommendations and strongly suggested that it should be expunged. They argued that if the clause were retained, a few disgruntled elements could always successfully apply it to remove an effective acting head of a department whom they disliked. They also threatened that if the clause were retained, they would amend it to affect even substantive heads of departments. They warned that the clause could become a double-edged sword which surely would be made to cut both ways.

Dr Jungu kept mute throughout the debate. Everyone was surprised, even though most lecturers knew that Dr Jungu must have been most pleased at the trend of the debate. They still expected him to say something, but he refused to comment. Dr Alamo's suggestion that the report be taken clause by clause and be voted upon was accepted. This was an opportunity for Dean Nada's supporters to muster support from those sitting on the fence. Dean Nada then surprisingly announced a fifteen-minute adjournment, a clever move that proved futile.

The 'experts' gathered together at one end of the hall in which the meeting was being held and must have resolved to vote solidly in support of Dean Nada's views. Dean Nada moved freely among staff members in an attempt to win many converts. He did not hide his feelings and for once he was rather blunt. Dr Jungu, on the other hand, sat quietly and still refused to talk to anyone. He was sure that his supporters would not let him down. The gong sounded and the meeting reconvened.

'May I have your comments on recommendation 1 (a),' announced Dean Nada. Clause 1(a.) and (b) were adopted by majority vote without much discussion. Clause 1(c) on the other hand became so controversial that Dean Nada decided to postpone further discussion on it to the end of the meeting. All other clauses also got easy passage through the meeting.

Returning to Clause 1(c) which dealt with the appointment of a vice-dean if the report was accepted, Dean Nada raised a technical point to the effect that the post of vice-dean was not statutory and as such could not be reacted until approval had been given by the university senate or by the president acting under provision 16(1) (d) of the University Act. Many lecturers countered this by querying the present procedure adopted by the dean in appointing acting headships or departments and acting deanship of the faculty since he did not also comply with the provisions of the University Act. Moreover, the dean was reminded that he himself had been occupying his post unconstitutionally, since the Act provided that he be elected by the members of the faculty and not appointed by the president as in this case. Sensing that a compromise was the only way to satisfy the faculty for that moment, Dean Nada agreed to submit to the wish of the majority. He then put the offensive clause 1(c) to vote and it was again accepted. Dean Nada then asked that someone move a motion to enable the faculty to accept and adopt the report. The motion was moved by Dr Alamo and seconded by Mr Nosiru. In the absence of a counter-motion, it was put to the vote.

108

Pieces of white paper were distributed and Dr Carpenter was asked to collect the ballot papers after everyone had cast his vote. Dean Nada decided to count the votes himself since he could not even trust his bootlickers. He was indeed opposed to the adoption of the Wusam report and he saw this as his last chance to achieve his objective. As Dean Nada banged the table with his gavel asking for everyone's attention before announcing the result, the atmosphere became very tense.

'There are twenty-three votes for adopting the report and another twenty-three votes against. Using my casting vote which I now intend to exercise, the Wusam report is rejected,' announced Dean Nada.

Dr Jungu's eyes suddenly turned red. He looked bitter and angry. He thought fast, raised his hand, and was allowed to address the meeting.

'Mr Chairman, I beg to move that the votes be recast. It would appear that we have some ghost voters in our midst since we appear to have over voted. We are only forty-four in this hall and yet you came out with forty-six total votes cast before exercising your casting vote. To some of us, it is not how the ballots go in that counts but how they come out. Although I do not wish to accuse anyone of rigging the ballot, I sincerely hope a recount will be permitted or the votes be recast.'

There was dead silence. A quick count of all present was made and the number of forty-four was confirmed. Anyway, there were only a total of forty-five members of staff in the faculty. Dean Nada became embarrassed and decided to apologize for the error. New pieces of paper were distributed and voting was done a second time. All the papers were collected and counted together first. There were forty-four. Thereafter, they were sorted out. The result was twenty-three for the adoption of the Wusam report, twenty-one against, and no abstentions. A loud ovation greeted the announcement and Dr Jungu's face glowed with delight. At least the voice of reason had prevailed.

Dr Jungu again asked for the floor to make a statement. Dean Nada, unaware of what Dr Jungu was up to, allowed this.

'I am happy that faculty members have been very patient, have persevered and are around to witness this momentous occasion. Although most of you would feel disappointed, I beg to announce publicly that I do not intend to contest for the post of vice-dean of the faculty. I want to be remembered as a man who fought for principles and not for personal glory. My mind is made up. Moreover, I cannot even condescend to serve as an assistant to Dean Nada. I have been pushed to the wall and it is high time Dean Nada was told a few home truths. He is a professor just like myself, and coincidentally neither of us is a head of a department. So it stands to reason that if the president would allow the University Act to operate, I could possibly get elected as dean of the faculty in a free and fair election. You all remember how he manipulated the vote count over the Wusam report. Does that befit a respected dean? It is even more mean for him to canvass that I should not be nominated for the post of vice-dean. He even went so low as to use some of you against me in an attempt to smear my good reputation. I want Dr Nada to realize that he must put an end to his antics, otherwise I will hit back and very hard too. It is shameful that people like Dr Nada fail to address themselves to the task of finding solutions to the many agricultural problems confronting this young developing nation; rather, he and his followers waste their energy on intrigues and living on falsehood. The day of reckoning has at last arrived for him. I hope Dr Nada will chart a new and worthy course.'

As Dr Jungu sank into his seat, everyone looked around in amazement. It was unbelievable. Dean Nada had never had it so bad.

'Any comments,' asked Dean Nada as he rolled his roving eyes from one end of the hall to the other, as if trying to force an answer from one of the people present. Not a word followed. He paused for a while and still there was no reply. Apparently confused and not knowing what to say, Dean Nada asked that the meeting be adjourned.

News went round the campus about the episode. Most people praised Dr Jungu's courage and felt that the time was long overdue for Dean Nada to be dressed down. Others feared that Dean Nada would use his close association with the president to get Dr Jungu out of the university. Most people, however, reasoned that this would be near impossible since Dr Jungu held a permanent appointment as a professor.

The messenger attached to the president's office was seen with some letters in the faculty of forestry and horticulture the next day. The president had invited Dean Nada and Dr Jungu for a chat. They both turned up at the appointed time. The president indicated that he had called the meeting to smooth relations between the two most senior members of the faculty. He revealed that he expected what had happened as he was aware of the tension between the two men for a long while. He stated that two members of the faculty had come to him on the day the Wusam report was submitted to the dean expressing fears that Dr Jungu might become vice-dean and later dean of the faculty. He stressed that Dr Jungu's complaints were founded, but that he did not approve of his approach in seeking redress. He therefore appealed to both men to forget the past and open a new chapter.

Dean Nada thanked the President for his timely interven-

111

tion, but implored him to allow him to state his case and call witnesses to support his arguments. He denied all the charges levelled against him by Dr Jungu and explained that he had refrained from answering the accusations at the faculty meeting so as not to make the situation worse. The president, finding that his approach would not satisfy Dean Nada, asked that the meeting should reconvene in his office two days later and that all witnesses would be invited. Dr Jungu raised an objection, insinuating that witnesses could be influenced before then. The president calmed Dr Jungu down by stressing that he expected both Dean Nada and himself to behave as gentlemen.

It was three thirty in the afternoon and Dean Nada returned straight to his office. Dr Jungu, on the other hand, drove to his house, to acquaint his wife with what had happened. The dean picked up his telephone and invited Dr Carpenter and Mr Wusam, his key witnesses, to his office.

'Sir, I have a class at four o'clock. I am trying to assemble enough specimens for the laboratory,' explained Dr Carpenter.

'Forget all about that class. I want you right away. Send a note to the students cancelling the class and arrange to have it sometime next week,' stated Dean Nada in a rage.

'I hope it's not anything serious, sir?' asked Dr Carpenter.

'Young lad, ask no more questions. I want you in this office as soon as you drop the telephone,' commanded the dean.

Mr Wusam and Dr Carpenter conferred in the corridor outside the dean's office thinking that they must have done a horrible thing. They were fidgety and completely upset. Five minutes had elapsed and neither Wusam nor Carpenter was in sight. The dean rushed out of his office and queried Amodu.

'Have you seen Wusam and Carpenter lately?'

'Yes, sir, they are around the corner.'

Dean Nada virtually ran to the corridor where he found

Wusam and Carpenter putting their heads together to mumble a few words.

'What are you up to? Must I wait for another hour before you report?' queried the dean.

'Sir, we were terribly upset and confused,' they said.

'Enough of this useless excuse, please follow me,' requested the dean.

'Draw up a chair each and sit round that table and listen carefully. You will be summoned by the president in connection with the misunderstanding between Dr Jungu and myself. You must deny that I ever asked you to either campaign against him or that your help was ever solicited by me in changing some aspects of the Wusam report.'

'You must also deny ever being friendly with me,' Dean Nada ordered.

'But suppose Dr Adams and the other members of the faculty that we have actually spoken to about Dr Jungu should come up with statements contrary to ours. Won't we be taken as unreliable?' asked Mr Wusam.

'My good lads, what do you lose by denying everything? I will lose if you should tell the truth. Please save my neck,' pleaded the dean.

'It's a bit...'

'A bit difficult? Or what were you about to say Dr Carpenter? Don't you appreciate the full implications of telling the truth at this stage? This will be like a dog eating its own vomit. It's a question of my dignity that is involved. Mind you, the promotion exercises are yet to come up. I will certainly play my part creditably then,' he assured them.

'It's all right, sir,' said both of them.

'That's not enough. I must have something down in black and white to strengthen my hand. Take these pieces of paper

113

and render your statements on them,' requested the dean.

The written statements of denial were handed over to the dean after being duly signed by each party. Pa Amodu was called in and instructed:

'Type one original and three copies of each statement. Please keep it a top secret.'

'But someone could spy on me while the typing is in progress, sir. Don't forget that Dr Jungu has his own supporters too,' explained Amodu.

'You used to keep such things secret, what is the problem this time?'

'Sir, can't the statements be photocopied? Remember the American Assistance Programme delivered a photocopying machine to this faculty yesterday,' suggested Amodu.

'Clever Amodu. You always come up with excellent ideas. Do as suggested, but please make only three copies of each.'

Amodu smiled and left the trio. He was delighted at the fact that he would do the photocopying unsupervised. He made sure he produced five copies of each; three for the dean and two for Dr Jungu. He hid the copies meant for Dr Jungu in his briefs and thereafter returned quickly to the dean's office.

'Wonderful,' stated the dean as the beautifully reproduced copies of the statements were laid in front of him on the table.

A copy and the original of each was given to Wusam and Carpenter, while the dean held tightly to his two copies of each statement as hostage. The dean thanked his guests and implored them to keep their word.

Later that evening, Pa Amodu sneaked into Dr Jungu's residence. It was past eleven o'clock and everyone was fast asleep. He knocked lightly at the front door and when this did not appear to register the message, he moved to the window of the master bedroom where he tapped the windowpanes repeatedly and whispered his name.

'Can't Pa Amodu choose a decent time to visit us? Doesn't he think we deserve a good sleep?' said Aida, venting her annoyance.

'Hold it, Aida. Pa Amodu is always helpful. There must be something very important, otherwise he wouldn't choose to come at this unholy hour. I will be back soon,' pleaded Onaola. Dr Jungu opened the front door, but did not put on the living-room lights on the advice of Pa Amodu. They went straight to the study where the old man unbuttoned his pair of trousers and dipped his hand into his briefs and brought out four pieces of paper.

'What are those?' asked Dr Jungu, frightened that he might have earlier used them to clean himself in the toilet.

'Million-dollar pieces of paper. You need them as evidence against the dean,' stated Pa Amodu with a reassuring grin.

Dr Jungu grabbed one and read quickly through it. Pa Amodu tucked a copy of the other statement securely into his hands and Dr Jungu smiled.

'Wonderful, Pa Amodu. You mean the dean has got these fools to swallow their words?'

'This is not the time to ask too many questions. Plan your strategy. I brought a spare copy of each statement which you will take to the president as if they were the only ones in your possession. You never know, President Oranlola might decide to destroy them if the Americans decide to put the pressure on. Keep your own copies at the bottom of your clothes box. They are very precious. I am off.'

'Immense thanks. I will forever treasure your assistance and loyalty. Good night, Pa Amodu.'

'What was the big news?' asked Aida, whose eyes became

115

clear when Onaola returned to the bedroom.

'Dean Nada has got both Wusam and Carpenter to make written statements denying all they had done and said on his behalf.'

'It is ridiculous! These guys have no conscience,' shouted Aida.

'Hush! It's almost midnight. Don't wake up our neighbours. Pa Amodu is reliable. As a good neighbour he is definitely more valuable than a faraway brother. Let's go back to bed, darling.'

The next morning, Dr Jungu got an appointment to see President Oranlola in his office. There he complained that Dean Nada was buying over witnesses and produced the photocopy of the written statements made under duress by Wusam and Carpenter as evidence. The president was shocked. There and then he assured Dr Jungu that he might have to adopt a new approach so as not to misdirect himself and deny justice to Dr Jungu. He implored him to remain calm in the face of this latest provocation.

The meeting arranged by the president with Dean Nada and Dr Jungu reconvened two days later as previously planned. President Oranlola made a surprise announcement to the effect that he had decided not to invite any witnesses as he did not think that that would resolve the misunderstanding.

'But this new turn will not give me an opportunity to fix Dr Jungu since he is unlikely to be able to make a good case. He has since grown wings and won't even submit to my authority,' cut in Dean Nada.

'And who are you - a worthless bungler of a Professor? Or a slave driver of a dean who is in Kato for a good time? The sooner people of your type pack out of here, the better for Kato, you lousy nincompoop,' retorted Dr Jungu.

116

'Enough of this trash and I hope you will shut your beak,' shouted Nada.

'I will give you a showdown if you ask for it, you lout,' answered Dr Jungu.

'Dr Jungu, remember that a push truck that lies in the path of an approaching train will be crushed to smithereens within seconds,' counselled Nada.

'Issuing your usual threats again? You are only a toothless bulldog. I want to remind you that I did not come here at your instance and I have no regrets whatsoever. It is important to point to one's antecedent to be able to get a good perspective on this problem. I came here with a good reputation and had lived in complete amity with all those with whom I had worked. Even here at Serti, such is the interest shown by various groups of people that I feel that my presence here could not have been without some merit. I feel proud of my contributions which speak for themselves during my short but profitable stay here. Whatever happens, I will continue to be reckoned with as one of the senior Africans in the field of forestry and horticulture. Although I feel deeply that I have not been treated with the respect and support that I deserve by you, hopeless man, I will continue to serve loyally and contribute to the development of the university,' concluded Dr Jungu.

'Mr President, I have had enough of this bodyliner. Dr Jungu ought to realize that I am still his boss by the grace of God,' stated Dean Nada.

In keeping with his exalted position, President Oranlola, who maintained a serene dignity throughout, called a halt to the unpleasant exchange and offered some advice:

'Gentlemen, wise counsel dictates that this misunderstanding be resolved before it degenerates into enmity. Please bear in mind that when two kids are trying to fell a big tree in a

117

forest, it's the elders who can predict precisely where it will land. A fight to finish will therefore not be in the interest of either of you. It will be a shame if I cannot settle this rift. I must confess that I have found myself in the unique position of a prosecutor and judge without a jury. The implications are obvious; it may lead to miscarriage of justice. Remember that the success of the entire faculty lies in your friendliness, unity of purpose and co-operation. I therefore appeal to you both to forget the past and disguise tactical retreats as victors. It pays to know when to call a halt to an ugly situation.'

'I promise to abide by your wise counsel, sir,' pledged Dr Jungu.

'I also accept your plea, Mr. President, and look forward to cooperation from Dr Jungu henceforth,' declared the dean. Pretending cheerfulness, the two men shook hands and the president praised them for being so magnanimous. He noted that that could probably be the beginning of a new and profitable era in the faculty.

118

8

INVITATION BY THE PRESIDENT

Dr Jungu had just returned from a shopping spree at Buktu. It was usual at weekends for lecturers to take advantage of their friends going to Buktu to ask them to buy some provisions for them. Dr Ernie Adams arrived at the Jungus' residence around seven o'clock that evening.

'Hello, Ernie, did you dream about Onaola's return? He returned only five minutes ago,' welcomed Aida.

'How about that? I know that he always comes back around seven,' remarked Ernie.

'Please be seated. May I offer you a beer?'

'No, Aida, I prefer some whisky and soda.'

As Aida opened the refrigerator to collect the ice-cold soda, a gentle knock was heard on the front door. Ernie opened the door and there was Brimah, the president's messenger.

'Good evening, can I help you?' asked Ernie.

'I have come to deliver this letter to Dr Jungu, sir.'

'May I have it so that I can hand it over to him later? He is in the bedroom changing his clothes.'

'No, sir, I'd rather wait. I have instructions from President Oranlola to deliver it to Dr Jungu and no one else,' replied Brimah.

119

Turning to Aida, Ernie asked that Dr Jungu be called from the room. Meanwhile, Brimah was offered a seat in the living room.

Dr Jungu appeared with his shirt unbuttoned.

'Nice to see you, Brimah. Any news from the boss?'

'Yes, sir. There is a letter for you.'

He grabbed the letter and tore it open hastily. He was not sure what the contents were likely to be. An invitation to drinks on Sunday evening, it turned out to be. What a pleasant surprise!

'Thank you, Brimah. Please convey my best wishes to the president,' said Dr Jungu.

'Good night, sir.'

'What's the big news?' asked Ernie.

Turning to Aida, he said that President Oranlola had invited him alone to drinks the next evening.

'Things are changing. In all my two years here I have never heard of an occasion when President Oranlola has invited a black lecturer to his house. Is he trying to win you over?'

'He is probably just realizing that he needs us as much or even more than the 'experts' The 'experts' are to be here for two to four years, but he is stuck with us for life,' added Dr Jungu.

'Can I have another whisky and soda, Aida?' called Ernie.

'By the way, I was unable to get enough beef for you from the Ministry of Agriculture, Forestry and Animal Resources meat shop at Buktu. Dr Harry got there before me,' stated Dr Jungu.

'You mean he bought it all again?' asked Ernie in anger.

'Trust him. He acquires enough meat to fill his two deep freezers. That's what money can do.'

120

'The earlier these 'experts' realize that we need the protein much more than they, the better for us.'

'Poor you. You might soon settle for the offal, as the price of beef will be raised by one hundred and fifty per cent from next week.'

'You don't mean it? Not even our British or other expatriate friends will be able to afford it. Who then will pay that prohibitive price?' asked Ernie.

'The American 'experts', of course. Did you not hear of the report of some American meat marketing advisers recently submitted to the Ministry of Agriculture, Forestry and Animal Resources?'

'And so what?'

'The implications are obvious. There is not enough juicy meat to meet the needs of the African elite and the American 'experts' in Kato. Raise the price to an unbearable level and the Americans will be the sole custodians of the juicy meat.'

'Professor, something is wrong with our policymakers. Don't they realize that the advice is not in the interest of the Africans?'

'Sometimes our people don't read between the lines. What was probably most important to the minister was the fact that the meat shop will make more money,' remarked Dr Jungu.

'More money as an invitation to kwashiorkor? The big shots won't even smell the disease. They and their families are privileged. They can buy from the meat shop anytime, but pay, if they ever do, a year later.'

'Ah-ha! Drop the chalk and turn a professional politician

121

too. You may be lucky to win a seat in the Parliament and be appointed a minister,' suggested Dr Jungu.

'It's almost eight o'clock. I must go. I am not cut out for politics.'

Ernie collected the items that Dr Jungu had bought for his family from Buktu and promised to return late Sunday evening to hear about his visit to the residence of the president.

Early on Sunday morning at cockcrow, Pa Amodu sneaked into Dr Jungu's house before many people at Serti were up.

'It's rather early, Pa Amodu.'

'You can be sure I wouldn't have come unless there is something special,' replied Amodu.

'And what can that be?'

'My intelligence source revealed that you will be visiting President Oranlola later today.'

'True enough. But how did you get to know about it?.'

'Well, Dr Adams talks too much. He was envious of the fact that while President Oranlola had never invited any senior Kato citizen to his house, he had considered it fit to invite you. I even heard him tell one of his friends that you too were to be watched as he thought you should no longer be trusted.'

'That's his own problem. Pa, let's talk more about my visit to the president's house. Mind you, I cannot do much here without your guidance.'

'Listen. You have to be very careful. President Oranlola is a clever manipulator. Let him do all the talking, but open your ears and eyes,' advised Pa Amodu.

'Must I not say a word? Won't he be suspicious?' asked Dr Jungu, taking Pa Amodu too seriously.

'Punctuate whatever he says with broad smiles and grin most of the time. If you have to say something, don't forget to be very polite.'

'What exactly do you mean?'

'As president, Dr Oranlola must be addressed as 'sir' all the time.'

'But the white lecturers have never been known to say 'sir' to him.'

'Dr Jungu, learn to take a cue from other black men. President Oranlola, like the 'experts', also operates on double standards.'

'Pa Amodu, suppose I choose to be different. Mind you, I am a professor, not just a lecturer like most other black folks.'

'Have you heard the saying: respect and worship those in authority? That's the least an African boss demands of his subordinates,' remarked Amodu.

'Respect them I admit, but why worship them? It's even more difficult to succeed among your own people. We have to please the white man and be servile to the African boss to succeed. What a life?' Pa Amodu interpreted the repeated nods by Dr Jungu as an encouragement to continue with his learned observation. He spoke again:

'It's you book people who should have changed the picture, but most of you like to be worshipped just like the white gods whose actions you all criticize.'

'You make a point there. I hope our people will listen.'

'Dr Jungu, I must take leave of you now.'

'Please wait for breakfast,' invited Dr Jungu.

'Let me slip out before I am seen here.'

'Please take a packet of cornflakes home for your break-fast.'

'What do you call cornflakes? I never saw a packet before. We eat rice and palava sauce even in the morning.'

Dr Jungu went quickly into the kitchen store and brought an open packet of cornflakes. He poured some of it on the outstretched palm of Pa Amodu, who shouted, 'Never! I cannot figure out how you educated folks get satisfied eating those light materials. My family will need to eat five to seven packets every breakfast.' Dr Jungu burst into laughter. He had hoped he could treat Pa Amodu like a special guest.

'Well, Pa Amodu, take this five dollars instead.'

'Thank you and good morning.'

Dr Jungu checked on the time every so often. His appointment was for four o'clock and he wanted to maintain his reputation for punctuality. At three thirty, Aida reminded him to be on his way. He pleaded that he would stay on till just fifteen minutes before the hour, as President Oranlola lived two kilometres from them. At precisely five minutes to four, Dr Jungu pressed the electric call bell at the president's house. He waited for almost half a minute before the door swung open.

'You want to see the president? Your name, sir?'

'Onaola Jungu,' was the reply.

'Sit down sir, he will be here soon.'

A few minutes later, President Oranlola strolled into the living room with a long American cigar in his hand. He puffed some smoke from the cigar and offered his hand to Dr Jungu to exchange greetings.

'Nice that you could make it. I feared that a previous engagement might prevent your coming. Please be seated.'

'Thank you, sir. And how is Madam?' asked Dr Jungu.

'Fine. She is away to Serti village with the children to see her sister.'

'I hope I will be privileged to see them before I go.'

'Definitely.' I intend to keep you for a fairly long time in your own interest.'

Dr Jungu adjusted himself in his otherwise comfortable chair. He was a bit disturbed.

'Nothing to worry about. By the way, what would you like to drink?' asked President Oranlola.

'Coca-Cola, sir.'

'Is that all? Please feel free and be at home.'

'That's all I drink, sir,' replied Dr Jungu.

The president pressed a bell and a steward showed up. He asked him to get a tall glass of ice-cold Coca-Cola for Dr Jungu and gin and tonic for himself. Before long, the steward reappeared with the drinks.

'Cheers!' called President Oranlola.

'To your good health, sir,' replied Dr Jungu as he raised his glass.

'Quite frankly, we are a bit worried about you,' Dr Jungu was told.

President Oranlola sipped a little gin and tonic and continued his observation. 'You seem to be turning into a fire-brand on campus. I appreciate your enthusiasm, knowledge, and sincere interest in the progress of this university and that of this country, but I am afraid you have to take it easy. I wish you were sitting on this hot seat as the president of the university. Many of you must be surprised at most of my actions and pronouncements which tend to favour our American friends. I assure you I cannot afford to do otherwise. Mind you, the first law of survival is that

125

of self-preservation. These Americans pay the salaries of forty percent of the staff in our biggest faculty, that of forestry and horticulture. They also finance the postgraduate training programme of all our assistant lecturers. To date, we have been lucky to have ten of them completing their master's degree, while another five have obtained Ph.Ds. In addition, they also supply much equipment, most of which I agree is a liability since they are either too expensive to run or there are no competent technicians around to operate them. From this, you will appreciate that my hands are tied. I have said so much to allay your fears.'I wish to assure you that you have my backing for all you have been trying to do to improve the organization and running of your faculty. Honestly, I wish to assure you that you have the freedom of the Serti campus,' concluded the president.

'Thank you, sir. I am most grateful for this honour and brotherly counsel. I cannot but think that I am like a guest who was given the freedom of a city while the key to the city was safely tucked away in the pocket of the host.'

'It's true I have the final say on all matters,' added the president.

'Feel free to come to me with your problems. It's not profitable to air them at your faculty meetings. You may not know it. Each faculty has a faculty advisory committee composed of heads of departments. They review all faculty decisions and make recommendations whenever they feel that such decisions are not in the interest of the faculty.'

'Ours is a unique situation, though. Mind you, sir, all members of the faculty advisory committee are Americans; all of them except one are junior to me,' observed Dr Jungu.

'It's a delicate matter. Don't forget that he who pays the piper calls the tune. You see, our Minister for Foreign Assistance signed an agreement with the American Assistance Programme without scrutinizing the provisions of the agreement. Please give me a minute to show you a few shocking things,' requested the president. From his study, the president brought two old files and put on his reading glasses. 'Please move close,' he beckoned. 'You can see that ten years ago when the first agreement was to be signed, my views were sought by the then Minister for Foreign Assistance. Then I advised that it was unreasonable for all the posts under the programme to be filled by Americans since I calculated that this exercise alone would account for seventy-five percent of all the money given through the programme. In addition, I observed that there was no provision in the said agreement to screen the qualifications and suitability of any academic staff to be recruited for the programme.'

'Sir, no wonder they sent you a mechanic who passed for an engineer in the wood technology department,' interrupted Dr Jungu politely.

'You are damn right. Now we are stuck with gunners, artillerymen, fitters, et cetera, in your faculty,' added President Oranlola.

'Can't you do something about it, sir?'

'It's difficult, if not impossible. I had another opportunity two years ago to advise our new Minister for Foreign Assistance on desirable changes to be effected when the agreement was due for review. Again my views were ignored.'

'You must have been fighting a silent battle. This is not

127

known to most of us. In fact, we hold a contrary view about you, sir. The nation should be made to know about this.'

'Be careful. Who controls the press, is it not the politicians? The new minister was given a conducted tour of Washington, D.C., and entertained lavishly when it was suspected that he might not sign his part of the agreement. Did you think he bought the Pontiac saloon that he rides? It was gratification from the Americans. We were definitely sold out,' lamented President Oranlola.

Dr Jungu shook his head and made a gesture of mild frustration. He thought the time might have come when he should become a sympathetic onlooker too. He thought that if the Minister for Foreign Assistance of Kato was not going to take reasonable advice from the President of Kato's only university on academic matters, he did not think it was fair for African lecturers to blame President Oranlola for all the ills at the university. Much as he was prepared to take lenient views of some of President Oranlola's actions, he was convinced that the president could have avoided a few administrative blunders if he himself had been ripe and qualified for the post of president which he held. President Oranlola's appointment was political. He was neither the most qualified nor the most experienced man around for the job. What operated in the minds of those who installed him was the current idea of ethnic balancing. As far as they were concerned, a coastal man had to head the institution. One should definitely treat President Oranlola's antics with the sympathy they deserve. He could not afford to lose his job since his qualifications and limited knowledge would not justify similar appointments elsewhere.

'You have now got an insight into our university politics,' added the president. 'Beware of the various groups on campus. You have five main groups: the Americans, other expatriates, the coastal and city dwellers of Kato and all the other Africans.'

'Am I not regarded as an expatriate, since I cannot represent the university at any conference to which Kato was invited?' asked Dr Jungu jokingly.

'You are really not an expatriate because you are not white,' assured the president.

'But, sir, head or tail, I lose: no additional fringe benefits, no special allowances, and yet I cannot attend professional conferences as a representative of the university.'

'You have my sympathy, but this cannot change overnight. I have prepared a memorandum on what you have just touched upon. The board of trustees has approved it: It is to be submitted for consideration at the next cabinet meeting as it affects our national policy.'

'There comes madam and your children, sir,' observed Dr Jungu. He stepped forward, opened the door and bowed as he said:

'Good evening, madam.'

'Good evening, Dr Jungu. I hope I am right. How is life treating you? And how are your wife and children?' greeted Mrs Grace Oranlola.

'They are all fine, madam, except for our younger boy who has fever.'

'Sorry. I hope you have been to the dispensary. Malaria is our number-one enemy here.'

'And that of the white man too,' added Dr Jungu.

'Grace, please take the children for a bath and prepare

them for bed. It's almost seven thirty,' noted President Oranlola.

'I must go home now, sir, I have had a most wonderful time with you this evening, sir. My discussion with you is an eye-opener. So there has been a lot going on quietly,' stated Dr Jungu, nodding his head repeatedly.

'Thank you for coming. Please feel free to visit us as often as convenient. My best wishes to your wife and I wish your little boy a speedy recovery.'

'Good night, sir.'

9

RETURN OF DR ADAMS

'Onaola, I see someone pacing up and down the corridor,' observed Aida from the living room, where the light had just been switched off as they were about to go to bed.

Dr Jungu moved toward the front door. He opened the door and asked:

'Who is there?'

'It's me, Ernie. I thought you people had gone to bed.'

'Not yet. Please come in,' requested Dr Jungu as he switched on the lights in the living room.

'Good evening, Aida. It's nice to be back here,' greeted Ernie.

'Please be seated. May I offer you your usual combination?' asked Aida.

'Whisky and soda, anytime,' requested Ernie with a smile.

'And what would you like to have, Onaola?' 'A Coke with plenty of ice.'

'Not tonight when it's so dreadfully chilly,' observed Aida. As everyone sipped his drink, Ernie asked:

'How was your historical visit to President Oranlola? –the first by a senior African at the university since its inception.'

131

'Most interesting and educating,' assured Dr Jungu.

'You mean that bum had something to offer? He is certainly due for a sack. I hope he won't be here much longer.'

'Don't write him off. He is probably on our side, but his hands are tied,' remarked Dr Jungu.

'Tied by who? Are you bought over already, or why these nice things about the unreliable and hopeless Dr Oranlola?' shouted Ernie in utter annoyance.

'Take it easy, mate. Why do you want to give yourself high blood pressure. Just listen.'

'Preacher, go on if you may.'

Dr Jungu took his time to explain what he had observed:

'I found the President is an innocent man suffering silently just like many of the Kato people on the staff of the university. He means well, but the agreement by the Minister for Foreign Assistance with the American Assistance Programme ties his hands. He is bound by the clauses of the agreement, most of which are stinkingly offensive.'

'You don't mean it. You appear totally won over by him. Has he promised you the deanship of the faculty?' 'Ernie, enough of that. You seem to doubt my integrity. You must know by now that I will never sell my conscience so easily. But we have to be objective. Give the devil his due. I repeat, Dr Oranlola means well. He may be limited by his inferiority complex and wish to cling to office at all costs. Can you blame him? Where else can he get such a lucrative job for a man of his limited experience and qualifications? He needs our sympathy, you know.'

'Pardon me, Professor, for being so harsh. I still advise you not to repeat all that you have said near your supporters. They will just not understand,' reasoned Ernie.

'Are you suggesting that they have lost objectivity? They must learn to keep an open mind on all issues. If I need to talk to them, I will not hesitate to do so. Dr Oranlola needs our help and cooperation much more than we need him. Life will be much better for all of us if we rally round him,' concluded Dr Jungu.

'I am afraid I must get out of here immediately. I would like to sleep over what you have just said. Good night.'

'Good night,' said Dr Jungu and his wife together as they led Ernie to the front door.

Dr Adams was in a bad mood on getting to his house. Not even his wife Linda succeeded in calming him down. He went straight to bed, but did not have a good sleep either. He was reported to have rolled from one side of his bed to the other and was heard by Linda mumbling a few words every so often. What Dr Jungu had told him that night weighed heavily on his mind. He dreamt about it all night. Next morning, Ernie left for the faculty offices, where he got a few of Dr Jungu's supporters together and told them what he had learned from Dr Jungu.

'I bet he never said those things,' remarked Mr Nosiru. 'It's impossible.'

'There must be some truth in what Ernie has just relayed to us. Remember, there is always some shred of truth in every rumour in Africa. Dr Jungu is alive, let's check with him,' suggested Dr Alamo.

All four of them went straight to Room 34, the office of Dr Jungu. He was just coming in.

'Nice to see you all. Any news?' asked Dr Jungu.

'We are here to see you in connection with your visit to the

133

president's house yesterday,' said their spokesman.

They repeated the version that Dr Adams had narrated to them earlier. Dr Jungu confirmed everything and added:

'Dr Oranlóla needs our loyalty, co-operation, and support. Forgive him for his past blunders. If we join hands with him, we shall triumph over the evil machinations of the 'experts' Please take my plea very seriously.'

'You are joking. How can you change so suddenly?' asked Dr Alamo.

'Gentlemen, you seem to forget the objective of the whole exercise. Let me make it clear that we are not fighting any individuals. We are fighting for principles. Dr Oranlola is not our target. We should be able to change the faculty organization without his support. If however he is made to feel that we are on his side at all times, life will be easier and the noble goal will be achieved much sooner rather than later,' he pleaded.

'There is no smoke without fire. Dr Jungu must have good reasons to implore us to co-operate with the president. Let's take his advice,' observed Dr Adams, who was becoming convinced about Dr Jungu's genuine intentions.

Mr Nosiru, apparently overwhelmed by some painful recollections of events on the campus, asked:

'Did you discuss why the board of trustees had not considered it necessary to curb the excesses of the experts?'

'And those of the president?' asked Dr Alamo.

Dr Jungu laughed wildly. He wondered what these people took him for. He suddenly burst out:

'That's ridiculous! Would you have dared ask the president such a question?'

He paused for a while, then continued:

134

'You know that forty percent of the board of trustees is made up of district chiefs who are only a shade better than illiterates. The few who are familiar with the workings of a university are often not invited to board meetings.'

'Sometimes we are told their letters of invitation to meetings are dispatched only after the meetings are over,' cut in Dr Adams.

'Surely! It appears you are familiar with the way the president and the registrar of the university operate. It must be obvious to you why discretion on my part was the better part of valour,' he concluded.

'Let's return to work before we are charged for dereliction of duty,' said one of them. One by one, they left for their various offices dissatisfied at the outcome of the dialogue between the president and Dr Jungu. As far as they were concerned, the important issue remained unresolved.

10

JUNGU MAKES NEW PLANS

It was June, a time for the college to close for the annual three-month-long vacation. It was not an auspicious moment for the African lecturers who could not afford a trip to nearby Ghana or even Nigeria, not to talk of faraway Europe or America. It was a different story for the 'experts' It was an eagerly awaited, delightful occasion, an opportunity to return to their home country for a joyful reunion with their kith and kin. But the 'experts' exploited this privilege, a special attraction in their condition of service, to greatest advantage. They invariably travelled home by the longest possible route. To them, this was an acceptable way to get to know other places; the cost of the journey being of the least consideration, since they did not have to contribute anything toward it. It was entirely financed by the American Assistance Programme as part of the aid to Kato.

At that time of the year, African lecturers were more interested in announcements concerning promotions and increments in their salaries. Recommendations had been forwarded by the heads of the various departments to the different deans of the faculties some three months earlier.

By tradition, a meeting of the faculty advisory committee of each faculty, consisting of all the heads of departments with the dean as chairman, met annually to determine who should be recommended to the board of trustees for promotion or for special incremental credits. This practice was never adhered to in the faculty of forestry and horticulture. The dean alone, but sometimes in consultation with each head of department, decided everyone's fate. This system was certainly open to abuse.

Speculation was rife about the promotion prospects of a few conscientious and productive members of the academic staff. The name of Dr Alamo was freely mentioned for upliftment to the rank of associate professor; that of Mr Nosiru, the hard-working, brilliant young man from Kato to the rank of lecturer, having been assistant lecturer for the past three years since obtaining a master's degree. Everyone was aware of what the other academic staff had contributed and no one could actually be fooled. For instance, Mr Wusam was notorious for returning in full, his research vote at the end of each session for the previous seven years to the dean. He never executed any research programme throughout his eight years at Serti. Rather, he assisted the dean in compiling students' grades in his capacity as the faculty academic secretary. Although this was a position not provided for in the statutes of the university, it was created single-handedly by Dean Nada only in his faculty. The dean had succeeded in attracting some non-monetary fringe privileges for the occupant of the position, such as membership on the Academic Board which was normally the preserve of academic staff of the rank of senior lecturers and above, heads, and acting heads of

137

departments. Mr Wusam felt ever so important as a special member of this board. He had a say in all matters which were tabled for discussion, but certainly not the vote. 'But whoever votes at Academy Board meetings?' was his prompt reply to anyone who dared taunt him.

Rumours were freely circulating that only Mr Nosiru had been promoted while Mr Wusam was granted a fantastic number of increments. This almost immediately generated some rumblings amongst the dissatisfied staff. Realizing that there was always some measure of truth in such rumours, Dr Jungu decided to check on the facts. He sought an appointment with the dean. This was granted. The dean confirmed to him the obvious, that he had been given only one increment.

'But this is contrary to your earlier promise made at the beginning of this session. You will remember assuring me of the maximum number of increments possible, in any scale of salary – which should be three in view of my very good work and contributions,' exclaimed Dr Jungu, tapping his head as if temporarily insane.

'Indeed, that is correct, but Professor Blake, your head of department, thought otherwise,' replied Dean Nada without any scruples.

Feeling completely dissatisfied, Dr Jungu asked, 'would you say the matter is closed? I thought as the dean of the faculty you are eminently placed to overrule the recommendation of the head of a department in your faculty.'

'Dr Jungu, I hate to do that. The matter could be reopened with Professor Blake. If your head of department is prepared to submit another recommendation on you for three increments, I will give my support to it. It isn't late since the board of trustees is yet to deliberate on our proposals. You have my permission to discuss the matter with Professor Blake if you feel so strongly about it.'

Dr Jungu was aware of the dean's initial diplomatic success, but felt that he should make an issue of it all the same, so that everyone could be aware of the arbitrary nature of assessing the ability of academic staff. He went to Professor Blake and requested a discussion on the same topic. Professor Blake, who seemed to be in a particularly happy mood and unaware of what had transpired between the Dean and Dr Jungu, welcomed the idea as he whistled his favourite song, 'O Lord here I come.' Dr Jungu, who was in an uncompromising mood judging from the frown boldly written across his chubby face, matched Professor Blake's humour by chanting in a low voice: 'Nobody knows the troubles I have seen.'

'How about that? Are we here for a revival service,' observed Professor Blake, taking the visit very lightly.

'You probably mean redemption service,' interrupted Dr Jungu, adjusting his belt and the sleeves of his shirt as if he was soon to engage Professor Blake in a duel.

'Well, take a seat, I hope it won't be a protracted session,' he said sensing some trouble.

Dr Jungu informed Professor Blake that he was advised by the dean to discuss his increment with him. He reiterated the dean's earlier promise of three increments and the possibility of reopening the matter with him. Professor Blake confirmed that he had recommended one increment based partly on Dr Jungu's contributions, but mainly because there was 'evidence of problems' on his part.

'Which problems?' he asked furiously.

Professor Blake explained in unmistakable terms that he felt convinced that he had taken a proper action in view of the problems that he (Dr Jungu) was having in certain quarters. He buttressed his stand by mentioning that he had picked up many adverse pieces of information on him from various quarters. He considered himself most considerate to have granted any increment in the circumstance.

'Do you realize that this is the first time such a thing is being brought to my notice? I shall be grateful if you would kindly cite an instance,' demanded a bewildered Dr Jungu.

'Ha! Ha! You remember the misunderstanding between Dean Nada and yourself?' asserted the head of department.

'The recommendations were forwarded to the dean …..?'

'Sometime in March,' interrupted Professor Blake, sporting a deceptive grin and not fully conscious of the implications of his answer.

'Would you be kind enough to indicate the time that the so-called misunderstanding between the dean and myself occurred?' demanded Dr Jungu, who was now subjecting his boss to a thorough cross examination.

'Er, er. . . around late April, April 30, to be precise,' he recollected. 'I knew about it officially though around May 5.'

You must be a vulnerable and not a venerable prophet!!' cried Dr Jungu, stamping the floor repeatedly with his left foot, a sign that he was becoming very impatient. 'The academic staff review and assessment exercise was done in March and you were in a position to foretell how I was to behave a month later? You must indeed be a prophet of doom,' stated Dr Jungu, pressing his advantage home.

'Everyone has his own way of running a department. I hope you will grant me this indulgence,' insisted Professor Blake.

'Leave you to continue bungling everything? Isn't it common knowledge that someone is not guilty until he is proved to be? If I were you, I would bring anything considered serious enough to affect the progress of a member of staff to his notice in writing,' he advised.

'You don't seem to appreciate that the walls have ears,' Professor Blake stated, laughing wildly.

'What? That isn't funny. You mean you hand down judgments on hearsay and gossip? Do you still insist on recommendations based on false premises?'

'Surely, but I needn't convince you on the soundness of my judgement. It has the dean's blessing, otherwise he should have overruled it,' insisted Professor Blake.

'We know how you all operate here. Your theme is: 'United we stand.' I have decided to render our exchanges into writing for record-keeping purposes. Moreover, I am aware that anything not written down cannot be believed. I will follow the normal communication channels passing it through you and the dean to the president. Will you assure its safe passage to the president?' implored Dr Jungu.

'Your petition will be promptly forwarded to the appropriate quarters,' he assured.

Within an hour of leaving Professor Blake's office, Dr Jungu had produced a carefully worded petition. He gave three copies to Professor Blake; one copy each was to be kept by the head of department and the dean, while the original was expected to carry the comments of Professors Blake and Nada before being passed on to the president for determination. It read as follows:

141

PETITION ON INCREMENTAL CREDITS

From:	Onaola, Jungu
To :	The President, Serti University
Through:	Dean, Faculty of Forestry and Horticulture
Through:	Head, Department of Horticulture.

It has come to my notice that some extraneous matters are affecting my progress in this university. After a detailed discussion with the head of my department and our dean, I feel constrained to place a few facts before you as both of them appear unable to resolve the matter.

From our exchanges, there are some elements of basic principles which I wish to bring out in the interest of fairplay:

a) That Professor Blake at no time brought to my notice, verbally or in writing any improper acts on my part, some of which he claims have affected his judgement in recommending only one incremental credit for me.

b) That Professor Blake was not in a position to fully assess my contributions, since he did not ask questions about my work. He has never visited my kola project

c) That I have established a kola farm without the benefit of a research vote from the faculty.

I feel strongly that Professor Blake is biased against me and that he did not address himself to the evidence before him. Further discussion with Professor Blake revealed that he is so prejudiced that he would use any information, no matter how it was obtained to ruin me without the courtesy of allowing me to either defend myself or to be given the opportunity to turn a new leaf, if the improper acts committed are of such serious nature as to affect my progress. It also became clear from our discussion that information collected, but which had no official bearing on my work, was being used against me.

May I crave your indulgence to make a few suggestions to encourage hard work and productivity and to ensure justice for all at this university. May I humbly suggest for your consideration that a form should be sent out to be filled by all academic staff to enable heads of departments to be fully aware of the contributions of their staff. The form should have:

Name, present status, salary, contributions during the year (to be filled in detail), recommendations by head of department and dean's comments.

There should be an avenue for redress in this type of circumstance and the impression must not gain grounds that only the 'good boys' get fair treatment and have a future at this university. As the head of department's recommendation seems to have been arbitrary, please find herewith an attachment showing my contributions to the university during the session just ended. I therefore hope that you will kindly grant the three increments, since both the dean and yourself are in a position to overrule a head of department, who may have committed an error of judgement as in this instance.

(Signed) Onaola Jungu
Professor of Horticulture

Professor Blake sat on his chair with his eyes glued to the ceiling of his office. He looked thoroughly confused. He did not expect Dr Jungu to go that far with the matter. He decided that he should rise to the occasion. He went straight to Dean Nada, spreading a copy of the petition on the table before him. As the dean browsed through the document, he nodded his head with a frequency similar to that of a lizard on its belly. He laughed loudly at the end, turned to Professor Blake, and asked:-

'Must we not reward those whose attitudes are characterized by a high degree of full-time commitment to the faculty politics and our success as experts in Serti rather than those claiming to contribute immensely to knowledge?'

'Yes, indeed, but you appear to be taking this matter lightly. With the contents in the attachment to the petition, any reasonable university president is bound to overrule our recommendation,' observed Professor Blake, looking rather upset.

'The easiest way to kill the petition is to prevent it reaching the president. You initial it and leave the rest to me,' the dean suggested.

'That's not fair. I gave my word to Dr Jungu. I would not want him to pick on me. I will be defenseless. Please, it must get to the president,' pleaded Professor Blake.

'Are you afraid of that braggart? Leave him to me. I will fix him. It should not be much longer before we frustrate him into resignation,' remarked the dean, unworried.

'That guy Jungu is indeed a man with lots of courage and iron will. I bet he will stay to fight another day. Ah, I remember now. . . President Oranlola should travel to America in another two weeks on a leadership travel grant. Let's put a covering

144

note indicating that you and I are trying to get our comments ready fairly soon to guide the president in taking a final decision on the matter,' suggested Professor Blake.

'That's a foolproof delaying tactic. You must have drawn on your many years of administrative experience to come up with that.'

They quickly got the note typed and signed. A dispatch clerk carried the original to President Oranlola, who was gracious enough to promptly acknowledge the receipt of Dr Jungu's petition with thanks. He added that he would be in a position to give a verdict as soon as the comments of the dean and Professor Blake were received by him. This was never to be, since no comments were sent by either of them.

Dean Nada sent his one and only trusted chief clerk, Pa Amodu, to deliver a copy of his note to President Oranlola to Dr Jungu in his office. It was also an opportunity for a dialogue between two good friends.

'Hi, Pa Amodu. It appears I am being kicked around like a football,' groaned Dr Jungu.

'This is not an occasion for many words. As an informed observer, I am in a position to give you the lowdown on the matter. Suppose we both ride in the mail bus to Buktu tomorrow, which is a Saturday? Listen carefully. Let's meet in the house of my uncle's brother at twelve noon,' suggested Pa Amodu.

'A perfect proposal. I'll be there,' assured Dr Jungu.

Aida advised her husband against making the trip to Buktu, stressing that it would be a wild goose chase. He did not heed her advice. He felt that he always learnt a lot from Pa Amodu each time they were together. This he considered most helpful for his survival at Serti.

The journey to Buktu was uneventful. Most of the people in the mail bus slept, as the journey usually started before daybreak. Pa Amodu and Dr Jungu sat so far apart that no one suspected that they had preplanned their journey together. The bus arrived in Buktu around eleven o'clock in the morning. Dr Jungu alighted before Pa Amodu. He did some shopping hurriedly and called a taxi which took him to the meeting place. He got there on the dot of twelve noon.

'Is this Pa Amodu's uncle's brother's house?' he asked.

'Which Pa Amodu?' replied a young man from the household.

'Pa Amodu who works at Serti University,' he explained.

'Yes, indeed, but he has not been seen around here for over six months.'

'He came to town today,' asserted Dr Jungu.

'That cannot be true. Pa Amodu gets here before noon any day he is in Buktu. You probably saw someone who looked like him.'

'Feeling dejected and about to give up, the image of Pa Amodu suddenly appeared like a ghost in the distance. It was not until he was about forty metres away that they were in a position to confirm Pa Amodu's lithe figure with a protruding stomach. His arrival was announced by the shouts of joy from all the children in the neighbourhood. Pa Amodu was certainly a man of the people.

'Sorry for keeping you waiting, Dr Jungu,' he apologized. 'You cannot visit your people without laying some small items for your uncles, cousins, brothers and all their children. That I hope explains my late arrival.'

'You needn't apologize. I feel relieved seeing you,' assured Dr Jungu.

Pa Amodu led his guest to a small parlour at the back of the house. He opened the wooden windows and dusted off the cobwebs, a confirmation of lack of use for upward of four months. He settled his guest in, but took time off to greet everyone and inquire about their well-being. He was most pleased to find everyone hail and hearty. His uncle's daughter, recently afflicted with elephantiasis, was said to be fully recovered. He summoned his uncle's wife and immediately instructed her to make lunch for two. She was to make rice and palava sauce, Pa Amodu's favourite dish.

'Feel absolutely free in this house,' stated Pa Amodu as he returned to the parlour. 'Shout if you like. No one is eavesdropping.'

'Thank you, Pa Amodu. Any news about my petition to the president?' asked Dr Jungu.

'With time you will learn to be less ebullient. This is one occasion when no news does not imply good news. Your petition is as good as killed. The president travels to America in another twelve days and he should be away for three months. Before returning, the board of trustees would have met to ratify all promotions and incremental credits. Dean Nada will be the acting president till the beginning of the next session. I assure you nothing profitable will come out of the petition.'

'Should I contact President Oranlola to brief him before he travels?' asked a bewildered Dr Jungu.

'The president can only make a promise. As long as the

147

experts are all one against you, President Oranlola dares not support you. Your petition is sure to be thrown out like an unwanted rag.'

'Who then were recommended for promotion in the department of horticulture?' asked Dr Jungu disinterestedly.

'Dr Carpenter becomes senior lecturer; Mr Nosiru is promoted lecturer; Mr Tando was raised to the grade of lecturer above the bar, what we refer to as lecturer Grade I, and Mr Wusam of course got six incremental credits.'

'Hold it!' he shouted in disbelief. 'Mr Wusam, six increments! How about that?'

'No wishful thinking, Dr Jungu. It's whom the 'experts' like, not what you know or contributed that counts,' counselled Pa Amodu.

'What's the fate of Drs Alamo and Adams?' inquired Dr Jungu, feeling deeply concerned for these conscientious scientists.

'They, like you, got only one increment each,' he stated.

'This university is bound to be plagued with staff instability. The qualified, able, productive ones are bound to look elsewhere for salvation,' observed Dr Jungu.

'And we shall be stuck with the boot-lickers and the unproductive lecturers,' added Pa Amodu.

'Shall we look on while Serti burns? Who will arrest the ugly trend, Pa Amodu?'

'It's you all, the academicians. To succeed, you will have to put your own house in order first. It is dirty. Remember that a leopard cannot change its spots,' assured Pa Amodu.

'Very difficult indeed,' confirmed Dr Jungu.

148

'The experts are not expected to change their tactics of divide and rule. They are united. You, my brothers, are divided into factions because of narrow self-interest which overrides national and other interests. Did you hear the latest pronouncements of Dr Adams since he got to know that he would have only one increment?'

'I hope he has not become indignant?' asked Dr Jungu, feeling sorry for Dr Adams's plight.

'He certainly feels cheated and thoroughly disappointed. He even regrets joining forces with you. He stated openly that he was being sacrificed. He swore never to be on your side again. He will probably turn a double-dealer like a professional politician who turns up with the party card of which ever political party is in power at the time of need.'

'It is a shame that Dr Adams has had to defect so soon. We are fighting for justice. We need everyone to succeed,' lamented Dr Jungu as he stood up to ask Pa Amodu to call it a day.

'Sit down, it is not time to return to Serti yet. This problem is of greater dimensions than you think. When I hear of these complaints, I look across the years and smile. The Democratic Republic of Kato gave these young lecturers and President Oranlola free education at the secondary school and university levels. It is a privilege denied many others, including my poor self. Rather than devote themselves to serving our institution and country loyally, they appear to be more concerned with scrambling for what they can get from the experts. Rules and regulations of the university are meant to be obeyed and enforced. Both Dean Nada and President Oranlola flout normal academic procedures and seem to get away with it. Not many people outside our campus are aware that our University Act had built-in safeguards to ensure its smooth running and justice for all, but it would appear that a clique made up of the 'experts' has taken over and does not want the university to run normally. Both the president and the board of trustees are answerable for failing to enforce the laws.'

He paused for a while and beckoned to one of his uncle's sons to bring him a keg of undiluted palm wine from the tapper next door. Pa Amodu served the frothing whitish drink in two big clay mugs: one for Dr Jungu and the other for himself.

'To your health and survival at Serti,' was Pa Amodu's wish as he raised his mug in toast.

'And your good health and long life,' saluted Dr Jungu.

Pa Amodu took a deep breath and applied his lips tightly onto the rim of the mug. The content of the mug was emptied in a matter of seconds. He breathed faster than normal thereafter.

'Pa Amodu, why so fast?' queried Dr Jungu.

He smiled and explained:

'I drink my palm wine. I don't sip it like the white man sips his hot tea. Your way of life has definitely been polluted by the white man's. I am an unadulterated African. I bet you shall continue to sip that palm wine for another hour .... Hey! Who goes there?' Pa Amodu shouted.

'It's me. Your son.'

'Wait a moment, Pa Amodu. So you have another son here?' asked Dr Jungu.

'Don't be funny. That's another of my uncle's sons. His name is Tolu. Remember in Africa, your uncle's sons are yours,' Pa Amodu explained.

Turning to the young lad, Pa Amodu commanded, fill that mug as many times as it is empty. OK?'.

'Yes, sir, but . . . .'

'But what?' shouted Pa Amodu as if already under the influence of alcohol.

Trembling and apparently frightened, Tolu was unable to complete his observation.

'Tolu, speak out. Do not be afraid,' assured Pa Amodu.

'Your friend's mug, sir, must I fill it also?'

'Thanks, Tolu. I should be all right with what I have,' replied Dr Jungu.

'You must recharge your mug. I hate to be accused of being inhospitable,' Pa Amodu shouted.

Although Dr Jungu tried not to incur the displeasure of Pa Amodu, he persisted in his refusal. He pretended cheerfulness and added:

'I am saving some of the space in my tummy for the rice and palava sauce.'

'Poor you, don't you realize that food and drink each has its own reserved place in my big belly? It is not a useless pouch, you know,' he assured.

Returning to the original topic, Pa Amodu spoke again at length, uninterrupted except for periodic breathers when he emptied another mug of palm wine.

'You all go on long holidays during the rainy season, a time when you as agriculturalists should be busy tending your crops on the field. The experts certainly like to enjoy the best of two worlds: avoid the unpleasant freezing wintry weather of their country, enjoy its bright summer season, but avoid our heavy rains. Why don't you advise the

151

board of trustees to change the university year to suit the economic needs of Kato?'

'Me? I feel elated.'

'I don't mean you as an individual. A collective effort by you and the other African members of the senate should achieve positive results.'

'You surely make a point, but who will bell the cat?'

'You, of course!'

'Pa Amodu, it's no use putting too many rods in the fire.'

'That's not all. Do you notice that every year, the 'experts' carry shiploads of soil away for analysis in their home country. Results from these have never been sent back to the university. It is an intelligent guess that they are probably prospecting for minerals and not trying to determine the suitability of our different soils for horticulture. One thing is obvious, the white man's permanent interest is in money, not in you or our country.'

'Pa Amodu, I share much of your views, but let's avoid wholesale condemnation,' remarked Dr Jungu. 'The bitter truth is that the masters that our erring brothers serve neither reckon with their existence nor count on them for their success. Our brothers toil to please the 'experts', but they are seen as mere tools for perpetuating their authority. The 'experts' expect our brothers to make peace with mediocrity and be used as a front to sabotage the efforts of the faculty. This is the crime of which I accuse my disloyal African brothers. I would have expected them to prefer poverty with honour to being down-trodden in guided affluence and servitude. Our brothers have chosen the latter course, an easier path to success in this context. Not many of us wish to suffer for too long. We are not used to making sacrifices in the overall interest of our mother-land. Ironically, just a handful of those who choose the path of honour ever make it and attain the peak of their careers. These few courageous men are our eternal inspirers. They will continue to kindle consciousness among the unsuspecting and whisper the words of encouragement into their ears saying: 'Fight on, brother, we shall overcome,' concluded Dr Jungu.

This train of thought lingered on in the mind for a long time. He was convinced that he needed the support of everyone, but he could not help soliloquizing:

'Poverty is indeed our greatest bug bearer. Most of our families are unduly large. This is a big bother and a source of temptation. In the words of a wise oriental: a large family is a tragedy for the children, a burden to their parents, and a drag on the whole society. Poverty has bred disloyalty amongst us and turned the weak-minded into stooges. Poverty with honour and self-reliance should stand us in good stead for survival in the face of constant exploita-. tion. We must make sacrifices to assure our children and our children's children full, satisfying lives. We should reject jobs for second-rate experts at the expense of some highly qualified Africans who are denied a legitimate right to acquire the much-needed cognate experience in their line of specialty. We have inadvertently not utilized the talents of our able brothers to the advantage of our country. It is probably true in our case that a prophet has no honour in his country. As human beings, I submit that we deserve equal and just treatment. We seem to be denied both, even in our country by our own people. In the words of an African head of state: "Africans have given the world

153

humanism, what we lack is technology". We need to acquire this in the shortest possible time. We need loans that can be utilized to develop our country in our own way, no aid in its present form. But first, let us learn to cut our garments according to the amount of cloth available. Only then shall we survive through thick and thin.'

Suddenly, Dr.Jungu recovered from his dream and said to Pa Amodu:

'Brother, I am going to continue the fight.'